STALKING HORSE

STALKING HORSE

George Pallas

SIMMS BOOKS PUBLISHING CORPORATION

SBPC

SIMMS BOOKS PUBLISHING CORP.

Publishers Since 2012

Published by Simms Books Publishing Corporation

Jonesboro, GA

Library of Congress Cataloging in Publication Data

2021907490

George Pallas

STALKING HORSE

ISBN: 978-1-949433-21-0

Printed in the United States of America

Book Arrangement by Simms Books Publishing

Editor Mary Hoekstra

Cover by Chester Hopper/Nichole Collins-Payney

DEDICATION

I dedicate this book to my wife, Sharon Pallas, and to my good friend, Laurel Beard, for their tireless assistance and invaluable suggestions that made it possible.

CHAPTER 1

The computer was slow. There are times when I feel as if I've spent my whole career, my whole life even, waiting for a computer to do something. Today was not an exception. Staring at the three screens on my desk had a hypnotic effect. Raindrops and possibly little sleet slapped against the office windows with a gentle patter that also worked to seductively beckon me into the arms of Morpheus. Since I had to wait for the running job to finish, I had to do something to keep from face-planting into my keyboard. I stood up, stretched my legs for a minute, then sat back down and rubbed my eyes.

Maybe I made a mistake when I was a junior at Franklin University. That's when I chose to change my major to computer science. Perhaps a career in law or education would have been more satisfying. It was hard to know and too late to do much about it anyway, but as I waited for my seemingly interminable job to finish, I fantasized about how other career choices might have played out.

Still no progress. I swore quietly but colorfully under my breath. Apparently, not quietly enough, though, because Rob in the cubicle across the aisle dissolved into a hearty chuckle.

"What's up, man?"

I shot a baleful glance in Rob's direction and grunted. My exasperation must have been evident because Rob apparently felt it wisest to leave me alone and made no further attempt at conversation.

Rob Ford is a smart guy. He's good at his job and knows a lot other stuff besides. He also has a wicked sense of humor that he displays often, and sometimes paralleling my own. He claims that he's descended from the Robert Ford infamous for gunning down the outlaw Jesse James. Neither I nor my coworkers had ever been able to verify this claim, but it makes for interesting stories around the proverbial water cooler, although CIS has, in fact, no water coolers, only vending machines.

Henry Ames, an analyst in InfoSec—Information Security—floated by and landed outside Rob's cubicle. I heard them droning on about one of their favorite topics, online video games. Their conversation continued until Rob packed up and left for the day, Henry tagging along. The two made an amusing pair. Rob was tall and had curly reddish-brown hair and a neatly trimmed full beard. Henry reminded me of a bowling pin, short and squat with sandy hair around the fringes of his mostly bald head.

My job finally finished just before five. Coincidentally, that was when Megan Simmons, my sort-of neighbor and carpool buddy stopped at my desk. She was ready to leave and so was I, but I had to tidy up a few things and fill out my time sheet first. I motioned toward my guest chair. She flashed me a smile as she sat down but I could see that she lacked her usual sparkle.

I returned her smile. "Rough day?"

Green eyes twinkled. "Yes, you could say that."

"Well, me, too! I'll be ready to bolt in a couple of minutes."

"Sure. Whenever."

A "couple" of minutes turned out to be closer to ten but at the end of that time I locked my screens and walked with Megan out to where I had parked my cobalt blue Mustang. I unlocked the doors and we got in. Our office building was visible through the windshield. "You know," I said, "this place has a disturbing resemblance to a federal penitentiary."

"I don't know, Greg. That big *Comprehensive Information Systems* sign makes it pretty obvious it's not a prison."

"Oh yeah? All it needs are some guard towers and a little concertina wire to fill out the picture."

Megan giggled. "Maybe you're right, but at least it's not like a prison on the *inside*."

I had to agree. The building's interior is bright and pleasant enough thanks to recent renovations. But Megan hadn't been with the company long enough to remember when the inside was as prison-like as the outside.

Columbus, Ohio does not have the traffic problems of, say, Los Angeles or Seattle or Austin, but driving at rush hour can still be unpleasant. By the time we had navigated our way from the office on Citygate Drive and approached the ramp to I-670 west, the heater in the Mustang was starting to overcome the unpleasant chill that had enveloped the city over the course of the afternoon. Megan sat silently in the passenger seat while I inched the car toward the highway and the wipers beat a regular tempo as they moved back and forth across the windshield.

We finally made it onto the freeway itself. As I eased into the main flow of traffic, Megan looked toward me. Her titian hair flowed down past her shoulders, framing her face. "It sounds like your day was kind of rough today."

"It probably wasn't as bad as I made you think. But I'd been hoping to get out a little early today, especially after

Brad canceled the staff meeting. Obviously, *that* plan failed miserably. Bummer of a start to the weekend, huh?"

"Yeah."

"How were things in the land of Desktop Support today?"

Megan didn't answer right away. Then traffic slowed to a crawl before stopping completely. Far in the distance, I could see flashing red and blue lights, which probably meant an accident was blocking at least part of the highway. We were at least a mile from the next offramp, so bailing onto city streets was not going to be an option. "Humph. Looks like we're stuck for a while."

Megan turned her body slightly, at least as much as she could turn while wearing a seatbelt, and completely changed the subject. "Liam and I had an awful fight last night."

I must have looked a little stunned because she quickly added, "We've carpooled for what, about two years now?" I nodded. "I think of you as a friend, Greg. Maybe it's because we shared all that car time and we've got to know each other. But I don't really have anybody else I can talk to about this."

So *that* was why she looked deflated this afternoon. Her comment about my day had been simply an icebreaker. I sensed she needed a sympathetic ear and uttered a simple, "Oh?" to encourage her to continue.

"Yeah. For starters, he came home half-drunk. I found out he blew off an installation appointment to go drinking with his buddies. When his boss found out, he suspended him for a week. It was his own damn fault, but *he* was mad at the boss."

Liam Murphy had been Megan's live-in boyfriend for about a year. Reasonably smart but woefully undereducated, he had perhaps enough ambition to fill a thimble. "Does he not get how upset people are when they arrange to be home for the cable installer and the installer doesn't show up?"

Megan looked down for a moment, then back up at me. "His boss tried to explain that to him, but he doesn't think it's a big deal."

"Does he still have a job?"

"Barely." Anger showed on her face. "They suspended him for a week without pay. That really pissed him off."

"Illogical, but I can see him reacting that way." Murphy always had trouble seeing anybody's viewpoint but his own.

"I told him he was irresponsible," Megan continued, "and he hit me."

"Hit you?" I exclaimed. My opinion of her boyfriend was that he *was* an irresponsible loser, but I never figured him for a woman-beater. Until now. "How bad?"

"He slugged me pretty hard in the arm and I had a nasty bruise this morning. At least with this crappy weather I can wear long sleeves."

"Meg, that's a serious big deal." Liam Murphy was a huge, powerful dude who could cause some real damage if he became violent. Megan was athletic but she stood little chance against this giant who was over a foot taller than she.

"I know, I know. I told him we were through and to get the hell out. He looked daggers at me, and, for a minute I thought he might really clock me. But then he backed off, packed a gym bag, and left. I hardly slept last night because

I was afraid he'd come back and *really* do a number on me, but he didn't.

"I'd been thinking about breaking up with him for a while, anyway. This just gave me the push I needed."

"It may not be that easy. Most of these guys don't take rejection very well. Has he ever hit you before?"

"No, this was the first time. Last night I was scared he'd come back and hurt me, but today I'm not so sure. Don't you think if he were going to do something it would have been last night or this morning? I did ask the building manager to change the lock, but he said it'd take about a week."

"It's hard to predict behavior in these situations. Yes, you'd think if he were the jealous, controlling, possessive type that he'd've never left last night. But you can't be sure."

"I guess not. But for all his faults, and he had a lot of them, I never thought of Liam as being controlling."

"Was he the jealous type?"

She looked thoughtful. "Not really. I mean, he'd probably be pissed if I went out with another guy, but other guys could compliment me in front of him and he'd just smile and think it was great."

That sure didn't *sound* like your typical abuser. "Now, you know if you call me, I'll be there," I said, although at the same time, I recalled that Murphy was 5 inches taller than me and his 235 pounds was mostly muscle. "But even though I live half a dozen blocks away, I can't be Johnny-on-the-spot. Is there someone in your building you could reach out to in an emergency?"

"Not really. You see, most of the residents are elderly and the few that aren't, are women."

By this time, traffic on I-670 had started to creep along again and I had to work my way toward the Third Street exit in stop-and-go gridlock.

"Now you've got me worried," I said. "Isn't there a building manager?"

"Yes, but the building's run by a property management company. The building manger is only there during the day; he doesn't live in the building."

"Well, could you at least let some of your neighbors know so that if they hear anything, they can call 9-1-1?"

"Yes, I suppose I could." Her tone gave me the impression that she was reluctant to involve her neighbors in her personal problems.

"Megan, I'm worried about this. About you. Promise me you'll enlist some of your neighbors to keep an eye on you. Have you talked to the police or thought about a restraining order?"

"Sure, Greg. And no, I haven't been to the cops and I've not thought about a restraining order. I doubt either one would do much good, anyway."

Maybe she was right, but I hated to have her do *nothing*. "I'd at least talk to the police, Meg. They might be able to give you some advice, even if there isn't anything they can do directly."

"I'll think about it," she replied.

"Meg, don't just think about it, *do* it." Megan was younger than my daughter. I couldn't help feeling and sounding parental.

Megan caught the tone. "Sure, *Dad*. I'll do that." Anytime I started acting or sounding like a parent, Megan would always bust my chops by calling me "Dad."

By this time, I had pulled the Mustang up to the entrance to Megan's apartment building. She hopped out of the car, grabbed her backpack, and gave me a cheery wave as she disappeared inside. I pointed the car toward my own condo and drove off.

Home at last, I parked in the building's underground garage. I stopped at the mailbox on my way upstairs. It contained nothing but a handful of junk mail that I would soon feed to the shredder. Opening the door of my unit, my Labrador, Champ, greeted me with his usual enthusiasm, his thick black Labrador tail whirling around in a motion that called to mind a helicopter rotor.

"Hey, buddy," I said to the dog. "I'll bet you're ready for a walk, aren't you?" It may have been my imagination, but I would have sworn that the helicopter whirled faster. I grabbed the leash, hooked it to the dog's collar, and said, "Okay, Champ, let's go."

If you have a dog and live in the city, you can't simply shove the pooch out the back door and say, "Shoo!" Dog owners in the city walk their pets on leashes. The responsible ones pick up after them, too. The rain had tapered off to a light drizzle by the time we got outside, but thick clouds still cast a gloom over the city and promising an early arrival of nightfall.

It took a few months, but Champ eventually figured out how to distinguish between taking a quick walk around the neighborhood to attend to bodily needs and a casual stroll for pleasure. With the inhospitable weather, this walk was going to be one of the former. In short order, we were out of the cold drizzle and back in the condo.

Like almost every other Friday night, I had nothing special to do. The weather made me disinclined to go out again, so I popped a couple of hotdogs into the microwave and made them my dinner. Then I settled into a comfortable chair and spent the evening reading the online editions of the Columbus *Dispatch* and the *New York Times*. By 10:00, I was nodding in my chair and decided to call it a night.

CHAPTER 2

Saturday was just as dreary as Friday had been although the rain had stopped. I took a quick shower before hitching the leash to Champ's collar. I tucked a yellow tennis ball in my back pocket with the idea of taking him to the Spring and Fourth Dog Park. Champ seemed delighted with the idea. He figured out where we were going when we turned left on Fourth at Long Street and practically dragged me the rest of the way.

We found the place deserted when we got there. The park sits on a wedge of land at the southeast corner of Spring and Fourth Streets. It's small, but there is room for dogs to run a bit. It also has a couple of benches where owners can sit if they're so inclined. Today I stood at the narrow end of the park and tossed the ball toward the wider end bounded by Fourth Street. Again and again I flung the greenish-yellow ball and Champ chased it down and brought it back, exhibiting the special delight that Labradors always seem to show. It's remarkable how much simple pleasure one can get from playing catch with a canine. Despite the gloomy overcast, I felt a sense of inner calm that helped me unwind from my work week. Finally, after almost half an hour, the dog looked like he had had enough. I pocketed the ball and we headed for home.

Back in the condo, I opened a can of Diet Coke before sitting down to one of my usual Saturday morning chores, paying bills. There weren't that many bills this week and soon it was on to the next weekend chore, laundry. I hauled a basket down to the laundry room, started the machine, and went back upstairs.

That was when I thought of Megan. After our conversation on the drive home yesterday, I worried that her doofus boyfriend might show up with mayhem on his mind. I had meant to call her last night just to make sure she was safe, but I forgot to do so. Now I punched the quick-dial button for her number on my phone. I hung up when voice mail eventually picked up. Megan rarely checked her voice mail, so I sent her a text instead:

Did everything go okay last night?

When I failed to receive a prompt response, I returned the phone to my pocket. *She probably has a busy Saturday*, I told myself but not very convincingly. An undercurrent of worry remained.

At lunchtime, a quick ride on the C-Bus, the free downtown circulator, landed me near Press Grill, where I ordered a club sandwich and a Budweiser. My table was up against one of the front windows, so I ate slowly, sipped my beer, and watched the people trekking back and forth on the sidewalk outside. Every so often somebody would stand out. For instance, the tall black man walking a large snow-white dog stood out. So did the young woman wearing shorts and a short-sleeved shirt, her tattoo sleeves on both arms and both legs, as well as her electric blue hair screaming "Look at me!" *She must be freezing*, I thought, since it was long-sleeved weather, but I guess she wanted to show off her body art.

My people-watching continued until both the sandwich and the beer were gone. I paid the tab, adding a generous tip. While I waited for the southbound C-Bus, I tried calling Megan again. She still hadn't answered my text and the call again went to voice mail. I tried text again:

Meg R U OK?

Megan still had not responded by the time the bus deposited me in front of my condo building. My level of concern ratcheted up a few notches because *surely,* she could respond to a simple text like that, no matter how busy she was. I decided to check on her whether she thought I was meddling or not.

Megan's apartment building was less than half an hour's walk from where I lived, and walking would make it unnecessary to hunt for a parking meter. I ran up to check Champ's food and water, then took the elevator back down to the lobby, giving him the run of the condo. Perfectly potty trained and long past the I-want-to-chew-everything stage, he is the perfect dog for a single condo-dweller. I never needed to put him in a crate.

I covered the distance from my condo to Megan's apartment in twenty minutes. I dialed her number once again when I reached her building and once again voice mail picked up. Megan's building, like my own, is one of those where a resident has to buzz you in to get through the outer door. She didn't respond when I pressed the buzzer, either. The fact that there was no answer to my buzz raised my level of concern a couple more notches. I took advantage of a small group of people exiting the building to slip in through the front door. Fortunately, they didn't challenge me.

I had been to Megan's apartment once or twice before, so it was not difficult to find her sixth-floor unit. The churning feeling in my stomach went into high gear when I noticed that her door mostly but not completely closed. I called her name through the door. "Megan! Megan! It's Greg. Are you okay?"

No response.

I tapped gently on the door. Again, no response. Knocking more vigorously caused the door to swing open slightly and a faint but unpleasant odor wafted out. Again, I called out, "Megan! Are you awake?" Alarm bells now clanged in my head. I gently swung the door open all the way and stepped inside. The door opened into a small entryway. I glanced into the living room area to my left and froze.

Megan Simmons lay on her back in the middle of a huge puddle of now-dried blood. She was naked, with her legs spread apart and her arms stretched out in a crucifix pose. What was obviously a savage beating left her once-pretty face virtually unrecognizable. My first impulse was to run to her to see if I could help. But I quickly realized that there was nothing that I or anyone else could do for her. Going near her would only contaminate the crime scene. I'm no medical expert, but my impression was that she had lain there since the previous night.

I wondered for a moment if Megan's killer might still be in the apartment and the thought raised the hair on my arms and the back of my neck. Unlikely, I decided, since the blood was obviously dried, and the nascent smell of death indicated that the killing had not been recent. He, and it was almost certainly a man, was more than likely long gone.

I fumbled for my phone and dialed. A female voice answered. "Nine-one-one, what is your emergency?"

"I want to report a murder."

"What's your name, sir, and where is the victim?"

"Greg West," I told her and gave her the apartment building's address. "Unit 613," I added.

"Is there anyone with a weapon on the scene?"

"I can't be sure, but it doesn't look like he's here. I don't think this is recent."

"Okay, sir. Officers are on the way. Stay there and wait for them. Don't touch anything."

"No ma'am, I won't," I replied and hung up.

Standing there waiting for the police, I tried not to stare at the nude body of a girl who could no longer cover herself. But I couldn't help noticing a colorful butterfly tattooed on her lower right abdomen about where her appendix would be. Megan had admired lepidopterans, so I was not surprised that she had chosen to celebrate them in that way. There was no jewelry visible. She had never worn much jewelry in the first place, so it was difficult to say what, if any, significance its absence might have.

Looking around the room, I saw considerable blood spatter on the walls and ceiling which I presumed, from the true crime books I've read and the *Forensic Files* episodes I've watched was medium-impact spatter from the beating she had obviously suffered. There was trauma enough to the poor woman lying on the floor. Other than the blood, though, the room itself was surprisingly neat. The furniture looked like it was all in its proper place and neither of the two lamps in the room were broken. In fact, the lights in both were on. The coffee table in the center was also undamaged, although a group of books and magazines that I assumed had once been on top of it lay scattered on the floor nearby. On the carpet near the body I saw a section of two-by-two, a length of wood soaked in blood. I judged the two-by-two to be about two or two and a half feet in length.

Megan's two cats, Smoke and Mimosa peered around the corner from the kitchen. Smoke meowed pitifully while

Mimosa arched her back and hissed at me before settling into a less hostile pose. They must be hungry, I thought to myself. Somebody would have to take care of them, but I wasn't sure if the police would consider taking the cats to be tampering with the crime scene. I decided to leave them as they were.

Suddenly, I became very, very aware of my stomach. It had been in knots ever since Megan had failed to answer my buzz at the front door. Now it was doing somersaults. Gastric discomfort increased exponentially with every breath of the death-fouled air in that apartment. *Shit! I can't barf all over the crime scene*, I thought. I quickly backed out of the apartment and gently pulled the door to without latching it, using my jacket sleeve to avoid leaving fingerprints on the handle. Away from the stench of the place, which had become more overpowering the longer I stayed in it, I managed to get control of my stomach before it decided to empty itself all over the apartment building hallway

Uniformed cops showed up minutes after I called 9-1-1. They looked briefly into the apartment but did little else other than start stringing yellow crime scene tape. Their job was to secure the place for the detectives. I noted approvingly that each of the officers kept their visual survey of the murder apartment brief; there was no untoward staring at the naked girl inside.

I had cooled my heels for close to an hour before two detectives arrived and introduced themselves as Sharona Vickers and Joe Tosca. Detective Vickers was a short African American woman. Her build reminded me something of a fire plug, yet overall, I decided, she was rather attractive. Her attire, a green blouse and navy blue or black slacks, was neat and professional, not the rumpled look I expected from a police detective. She wore her hair in a short afro style reminiscent of the 1970s, although she managed to make the look seem fresh and modern. Horn-rimmed glasses with oversized lenses gave her an inquisitive, intelligent look. I judged her to be middle-aged, probably somewhere in her mid-forties.

Tosca, on the other hand, was your stereotypical detective. He wore a rumpled gray jacket and a white shirt that looked as if he had slept in it. He wore no tie. He matched my 6'2" height but was at least 25 pounds lighter, his wiry frame giving off an aura of concealed power. He looked as if he had been constipated since high school and I guessed that he probably had an ulcer.

I decided that Detective Vickers was in charge. Maybe it was her demeanor, maybe it was the glasses. I couldn't be sure. Tosca gruffly told me to wait downstairs while the two of them started the crime scene technicians on their work of photographing, processing, and collecting evidence. I found what I decided was the least uncomfortable chair in the building's lobby. More of my Saturday afternoon ticked away while I waited. But it wasn't like I'd be doing anything else after witnessing that scene in Megan's apartment. That was one of those things you can't unsee.

It is a bit ironic that while the police question multiple suspects separately, they usually gang up multiple cops on the people they are questioning. It makes good sense to separate suspects so they can't coach each other and tailor their answers to each other's stories. What I never could quite understand, though, was why ganging up on an interviewee was supposed to produce better results. Yet, true to form, both detectives descended on me. The first questions were routine: name, address, contact information. Then they got down to business.

"How do you know the victim," Detective Tosca asked.

"The victim," I said, "has—had—a name. She was Megan Simmons. Megan and I worked together and carpooled together."

"When was the last time you saw her?"

"Yesterday afternoon when I dropped her off at her apartment building here."

"And you didn't see her or talk to her after that?" Tosca's demeanor was taking on a slightly accusatory tone.

"No, I didn't."

"You called her three times," he fired back.

"I *tried* to call her. I assume you know this from checking her cell phone. You should be able to see that none of those were answered."

"And you texted her. Why all the interest in someone you just carpool with?"

"She was more than a carpool buddy. She was a coworker and a friend. I was concerned because she mentioned that she'd had a fight with her boyfriend and said that he hit her."

Both detectives raised their eyebrows. "When did she have this fight?" Detective Vickers asked. She had a smoother, more sympathetic manner. They could have been playing good-cop, bad-cop, but I decided that the real difference was that Vickers had more experience as a detective, which is probably why, I assumed, she was in charge.

"She told me about it on our drive home from work Friday. According to what she said, they would have had the fight Thursday night. He almost lost his job, came home drunk, and they got into a verbal fight that turned physical when he popped her. She threw him out after that."

Vickers and Tosca glanced at each other as they considered the significance of this scenario. "What's the boyfriend's name?" Tosca snapped. "Where does he live?"

"His name is Liam Murphy," I replied, "and until Thursday, he lived here, with Megan. I have no idea where he went after she kicked him out."

Vickers motioned to a uniformed officer standing nearby and said something to him that I couldn't quite hear. I presumed it was instructions to have Mr. Murphy apprehended. Tosca, however, wasn't ready to let me go that easily. "Where were *you* last night and this morning?" he asked.

"I was at home last night," I replied. "I spent the evening reading a couple of newspapers online then went to bed fairly early. This morning, I took my dog to the Spring and Fourth Dog Park. Then I rode the bus up to the Short North where I had lunch at Press Grill. When I couldn't get hold of Megan, I decided to come check on her."

"So, last night, you didn't go out and nobody saw you?" It was less of a question and more of a thinly veiled accusation.

"Not last night, no."

"How about today? Think anybody at the restaurant would remember you?"

"Somebody might remember me, maybe the server, I'm not sure."

"Pretty weak for an alibi." Tosca had dropped the veil and was pointing the proverbial finger directly at me.

"I suppose so. Not knowing I would need an alibi, I didn't worry about getting one. But look here, Detective Tosca, Megan was my friend. I had no reason to hurt her."

The detective's silence spoke volumes. Then, "Who *do* you know that might have wanted to harm the victim."

"*Megan*," I said, emphasizing her name to remind Tosca she had one, "was a likeable person who was friends with just about everybody. I never heard anybody say anything bad about her. Other than the boyfriend, I don't know of anybody she ever argued with."

"*Somebody* must have had a beef with her," Tosca said, gesturing toward the door of Megan's apartment.

"Obviously. But I don't have a clue who it could be unless it was Murphy."

"What was the name of that waitress at the grill?"

The check and credit card receipt were still in my pocked. By checking them, I was able to provide a name. "Susan B."

Tosca scowled. I decided that must be his default expression. "I'll check it out."

Vickers rejoined the interrogation, saying, "Mr. West, we would like you to come to headquarters and make a formal statement."

Okay, I could do that easily enough, I thought. Headquarters was just a few blocks away on Marconi. "Yes, ma'am. When do you want me?"

"How about nine o'clock Monday morning."

"Sure," I said, thinking, *Another workday shot to hell.* "No problem, I'll be there."

"Thank you." Vickers, at least, was handy with the social graces, unlike her younger but more curmudgeonly partner.

I walked out of the apartment building and started walking back home, free as the air, at least for now.

CHAPTER 3

Champ vigorously rotated his tail in greeting when I opened the door of the condo. He was obviously ready for his evening walk. We took a short one up Long Street to Third and back again.

Daylight was mostly a memory when we got back. Depressed and in no mood to go out, I rummaged through the refrigerator and pulled out the carcass of a pizza I had on Thursday. Tonight's dinner was going to be the remnants of a large pepperoni, sausage, mushroom, and anchovy pie.

I thought about reading and thumbed through the titles in my Kindle library. But the combination of Megan's murder and the dystopian novel I had recently finished, Orwell's *Nineteen-Eighty-Four*, left me in no mood to read.

I decided a cocktail was in order. Setting the Kindle aside, I went to the kitchen, flipped on the lights, and took two bottles out of a cupboard. One was a blue bottle of Bombay Sapphire gin; the other was vermouth. I retrieved my cocktail shaker from the sink. Swirling hot water and dishwashing liquid around in it should make it clean enough, I decided. Ice from the refrigerator dispenser clanked into the shaker, then rattled as I gently shook the gin inside. Like James Bond, I preferred my martinis shaken, not stirred, even though some purists insist that by shaking, you bruise the gin. Seriously? How the hell can you bruise gin?

Taking a frosted martini glass from the freezer and swirling a little vermouth around in it, I filled it almost to the top with chilled gin and garnished with two large pimento-stuffed olives. I turned out the kitchen lights, went to the living room, and sat down in one of my comfortable chairs, and took a sip. Perfect.

My eyes fell on the small, framed photograph on the side table. It was a picture of Lisa taken shortly before she died. Her warmth and love of life radiated from the photograph. Even in her early fifties, her hair was still brunette without a hint of gray. Her eyes sparkled and I could almost hear her laughing. I kept another, larger picture of her from our wedding in the bedroom.

I bought the condo after Lisa died. Although she had never lived with me in here, her presence seemed to permeate the place, nonetheless. I had some other pictures of her besides the two framed ones, of course, but it was more than that. I got most of the furniture in the place after I moved in but there were still plenty of things she and I had shared: sheets, bedspread, bath towels, dishes. The list went on. Even the shaker I used to make my martini reminded me of her. She had given it to me as a birthday gift only a few weeks before her death.

Champ must have sensed the angst because I soon noticed a pair of sympathetic brown eyes looking up at me as he rested his muzzle on my lap. I scratched him behind the ears and took a larger sip of the martini. One of the wonderful things about dogs is their apparent ability to sense your mood and your pain. By nuzzling up to me, Champ was offering his sympathy and companionship.

I turned out the lights. This was going to be a night of brooding.

When I met Lisa, she was 20 and I was 24. We were both graduate students at Xavier University in Cincinnati. Lisa had gone directly from Ohio State to graduate school. It took me a little longer than usual to finish my own undergraduate studies because I changed my major a couple of times. Then I had worked full-time for two years before signing up for post-graduate studies. I naturally noticed the pretty, petite brunette who shared some of my classes. She had soulful brown eyes, a ready smile, and dimples. The other guys in the program, the straight ones, anyway, noticed her, too. For reasons that I was never able to fathom, she hung around with me. Over time, our friendship grew into something much more serious. We married two years later in the summer before our last year of graduate school.

I sighed as I sat there in the dark. The martini glass was empty. I turned on the lights while I made another one, then turned them out again and went back to my chair, Champ lay on the floor close by.

Over nearly thirty years of marriage, Lisa and I never had an argument or even a serious disagreement. We each had our own tastes, likes and dislikes, but we also had an incredible lot in common. We raised our son, David, and our daughter, Heather, with what I consider more than usual success. Both were on their own now, supporting themselves and thriving in happy, stable relationships. Lisa and I were beginning to enjoy a life of travel and adventure, free of the day-to-day responsibilities of parenthood, and planned to continue in that mode until age forced us to finally settle down.

I was working at my desk at CIS when I got *The Call*. I would always think of it as *The Call*, a telephone call that shattered my comfortable and secure world to flinders. When I answered the phone, a voice on the other end identified herself as a sergeant with the Columbus Police Department. She told me that there had been an accident, and that I needed to come to the Grant Hospital emergency room right away. She wouldn't tell me anything else. I have a dim recollection of racing downtown, clearly in excess of the posted speed limit. The memory of what transpired inside the ER, though, carved itself permanently into my brain. A uniformed cop and a woman in green scrubs greeted me, sat me down, and told me that Lisa was dead. She was crossing Grant Avenue on her way to meet some friends for lunch. A motorcycle roaring down Grant blew through a red light and knocked her down. She probably died instantly, the woman said in a sympathetic voice, but the ambulance brought her to Grant to see if there was a possibility of reviving her or keeping her alive. There wasn't.

The next few days are a blurry potpourri of memory fragments. Without warning or preparation, the kids and I had to plan a funeral. There was the usual outpouring of sympathy from friends and colleagues. As executor, I had to attend to the details of Lisa's estate. And each night, I came home to the empty house we had shared and cried. Concerned about my mental stability, my son, David, strongly encouraged me to find another place to live.

Although Lisa and I seldom disagreed over consequential matters, one of the very few things we *had* differed on was our preference for where to live. Lisa grew up in the suburbs and loved the suburban milieu. I, on the other hand, consider myself more of an urbanite. I like the hustle and bustle of city life. I did feel that the suburbs were a better place to raise children, but now that David and Heather were on their own, the 'burbs no longer held much attraction for me. After Lisa's death, it was an easy decision to sell the house, downsize, and move downtown.

I made another martini.

Moving was not easy but it did help. Leaving Lisa behind, as I was finding, was incredibly hard. I still missed Lisa, and many things around the condo still reminded me of her, but the paralyzing grief afflicted me less often. There were still exceptions. Tonight was one of the exceptions.

At this point, four years after I lost her, I would have welcomed a relationship like the one I'd had with Lisa. The thought of *dating*, however, left me cold. I didn't even know how to meet single, age-appropriate women. What was I supposed to do, join an internet dating service? *That* idea certainly didn't appeal to me. Since most people my age are either not interested or already paired up, I was at a loss as to how to go about meeting someone.

A faint glow from the streetlights ten stories below was the only light visible. *No moon on this overcast night*, I thought. But thinking was now something of an effort and my consumption of the martini tended to be more slurping than sipping. Champ came over. It was difficult to see a black dog in the dark room, but his pink tongue flashed in and out as he gently licked my left hand.

"Thassha good dog. Yeah, *goood* dog," I slurred.

CHAPTER 4

My head was stuck inside a carwash. The wet brushes beat against my face and something had me pinned so that I couldn't extract myself. Gradually, the scene cleared, and I realized that the wet brushes were not a carwash but Champ's tongue. His right paw rested on my shoulder as he vigorously licked my face. It was late Sunday morning and the sun shone brightly outside for a change, but I felt like hell.

Surveying the scene, the nearly empty bottle of Bombay Sapphire told me that I must have made another martini or two. My position told me that I had crashed on the sofa. Swinging my legs onto the floor, I slowly stood up. I rarely have a headache with gin, but I was plenty foggy and my gait none to steady as I hitched the leash to Champ's collar and headed for the door. No matter my condition, the dog still needed to go out. Our walk may have been slower than usual, but it served its purpose.

Lunchtime found me at the sushi joint on Third, where I ordered a beef Ramen bowl. A bowl of soup and soft noodles seemed more appropriate than anything else right now. That reasoning must have been correct because the Ramen bowl had the soothing effect I'd hoped for. I started to feel better, especially after gobbling a handful of Excedrin.

Hangover or no, there were still plenty of routine chores to do. The condo needed a good scrub. I hauled out the vacuum and the duster and went to work. I could hire a cleaning service, but it didn't seem worth it with just me living there. Besides, my weekends were mostly free, leaving me plenty of time to do my own housekeeping.

Even this chore reminded me of Lisa. After the kids moved out, she and I used to clean the house together. I grumbled about all the extra rooms we had to clean while she reveled in keeping our home shipshape. In the suburbs, there was also the lawn. I never did like yard work and taking care of that damned lawn was one thing I *certainly* didn't miss when I moved downtown.

It took me less than an hour to vacuum and dust the condo. Cleaning the shower and bathroom took a little longer. Nevertheless, I had plenty of time to do something after I finished. I did nothing instead. Reading still didn't appeal to me today, and I'd already taken Champ out. I decided to listen to podcasts for a while since I had an overabundance of episodes downloaded but had not listened to yet. I chose *Southern Fried True Crime*. Its episodes are about forty-five minutes to an hour long. I had listened to three or four when I decided it was time to take Champ up to Goodale Park, where he could get a good run chasing a frisbee. I snapped on his leash, grabbed the frisbee, and we started for the elevator.

I saw my neighbor, Jenna Stone, coming down the hallway carrying a trash bag to the garbage chute at the end of the hall. Jenna moved into a unit down the hall from me about six months ago. As neighbors, we frequently ran into each other casually. Some of those meetings turned into rather lengthy hallway conversations, and I had also seen her at some of the building's social events. She was pretty and intelligent and carried an air of sympathy and caring about her. Perhaps being a cardiac nurse at St. Agatha Hospital explains the aura of caring. Or maybe she's just a nice person.

Despite my rocky start to the day, I put on a smile and tried to sound casual. "Hey, Jenna, what's shaking?"

"Oh, Greg," she said, "I heard about that woman on the radio. They had one of those 'breaking news' bulletins and they said *you* found her. Is that true?"

"Yes, it is." I replied succinctly, not wishing to relive yesterday's horrors. I'd have to do that tomorrow for the detectives as it was.

She put her hand on my arm. "Oh, that must have been *terrible!* How well did you know her?"

"We worked for the same company and carpooled for almost two years, or so, so pretty well."

"I can't even imagine how you must feel right now."

"Pretty lousy, actually, and I have to give a formal statement to the police tomorrow, so that means I'll have to go over it all again."

Jenna's grayish blue eyes reminded me of a Himalayan cat. They were intense and now focused totally on me. I found that both flattering and a little uncomfortable at the same time. It was almost as if she had X-ray vision into my soul.

"Oh, I'm *so* sorry," she said. Her voice contained genuine sympathy. "You know you can talk to me any time I'm not working."

"Yes, I know that Jenna, and thank you. It means a lot." It *did* mean a lot, and it might mean more after tomorrow's session with detectives Vickers and Tosca.

"I'm serious. You know I'm just down the hall."

"Yes, Jenna, I do. Thank you. I really do appreciate you being there."

We parted. Champ and I walked to the elevator and Jenna headed for the garbage chute.

Goodale Park is a large park bounded by Goodale Street on the south, Victorian Village on the north, and Park Street on the east. Its namesake is Lincoln Goodale, the first physician to live in Columbus back in the early 1800s and the city's first millionaire. He was also a noted benefactor to the city. Young parkgoers can enjoy the playground while older visitors can take advantage of the basketball court or one of several tennis courts. A small pond in the park's northeast corner boasts a gazebo and, in summertime, a fountain with two baby elephants spraying water from their trunks. Since it is near the Short North district, the park is easily accessible to downtown residents by walking or taking the C-Bus, the free bus that circulates up and down High Street. I thought the Central Ohio Transit Authority might frown on a dog on the bus that wasn't a bona fide service dog, so I opted for walking.

The lovely, mature trees that cover much of the park's land were mostly bare this time of year, but Champ and I didn't mind. Out in the open air and sunshine, I threw the frisbee and he brought it back time and again until he laid down beside me, panting. I opened the bottle of water I'd brought for him and he drank it, sloppily. When the bottle was empty, Champ's muzzle was wet, but the water had quenched his thirst. I sat down and let him lie beside me while he napped in the midday sun. After all, he had done all the work. I just tossed the frisbee; he had been the one to chase it and fetch it back.

I decided I was still in shock from the horrors of Saturday. I thought about poor Megan, lying on the cold floor, exposed, literally beaten to death. I shuddered. It was almost impossible to get that image out of my brain, so I decided to see if I could find cloud animals in the puffy cumulus floating above. I imagined I saw elephants, lions, sheep, and a clown or two in the cottony white shapes floating lazily by. Champ snoozed beside me on the ground.

After about half an hour, Champ raised his head and gave me a doggy smile. I scratched him lightly behind the ears and his thick tail began to beat a slow tattoo on the ground. "C'mon buddy," I said to him, "time to go home." I stood up, fastened the leash, and started walking back to the condo. The helicopter was in full rotation now.

I needed to call my manager, Brad Carter, and tell him I wouldn't be in the office tomorrow. I dialed and he picked up right away.

"Hello."

"Hi, Brad, it's Greg West."

"Yes, Greg, what's up?"

"I've got a bit of a problem. You know Megan Simmons, works in Desktop Support?"

"Yeah, I think I've met her."

"Somebody murdered her Friday night, and I found the body." There was a gasp on the other end of the line. "The thing is, I have to go to police headquarters tomorrow morning and give a statement. And I seriously doubt I'm going to be able to focus on work, so I need to take the day."

Brad hesitated but only for a moment. I could see him rubbing his left hand over his bald head, which he had a habit of doing when he was nervous. "Sure, Greg, no problem. Of course. You *have* to meet with the police, and I bet you wouldn't be very productive after that. I know you've got plenty of PTO."

"Thanks. I'll see you Tuesday."

"Sure. And good luck tomorrow."

"Okay. Bye."

We hung up and I started trying to imagine just how tomorrow's meeting with the detectives would go.

CHAPTER 5

Columbus looked gray and tired Monday morning. There was no rain in the forecast, so I left my umbrella at home and strode towards the large police headquarters building at the corner of Marconi and Long. I covered the short distance in under ten minutes without having to hurry and was in the lobby before the appointed nine o'clock hour. An attractive young Hispanic-looking woman in an impeccable patrol officer's uniform manned the reception desk. I stated my business and soon found myself in an interview room awaiting the arrival of Detectives Vickers and Tosca. I didn't have to wait long before Tosca entered the room sans Vickers. I guessed that her absence meant that she had sent Tosca to have a run at me while she watched the show on a video monitor in another room.

I tried to brighten the mood with my cheeriest, "Good morning!" It didn't work.

Tosca grunted a reply, sat down, and plowed into business. "Tell me again how you knew the dead girl," he said.

So much for pleasantries or small talk. "Like I told you Saturday, we worked together and, since we both lived downtown, we carpooled together. Her car was, shall we say, unreliable, and I offered to carpool."

"How long you been doing that?"

"Carpooling with Megan? Almost two years, I think."

"How well did you know her?"

"We were friends. Not bosom buddies or lovers. Just friends. You can't spend 15-20 minutes twice a day in a car with someone without getting to know them."

"You two have a romantic relationship?"

Ah, there it was. "No," I replied slowly, "there was nothing romantic or intimate, just friends."

"Friends with benefits?" he leered.

"Definitely not."

"How'd you feel about that?"

I was growing increasingly uncomfortable with the direction this interview was taking. "I'm not sure what you're getting at," I said, knowing full well what he was getting at.

"Did you want to fuck her?" Ouch! *That* was direct.

"Megan was an attractive young woman and I'm almost a senior citizen. Even if I *had* considered having an intimate relationship with her, she would probably have laughed at me."

"So, she turned you down?"

I really didn't like the accusation in *that* question. "No, she didn't because I didn't ask."

Tosca glared at me. "That's hard to believe."

"Well, it's true."

Tosca let that float on the air while he scribbled in his notebook. Then he resumed the attack. "Here's what I'm thinking. I'm thinking you had the hots for her and tried to do something about it. She turned you down cold, and maybe laughed at you in the bargain like you said. You got pissed off and clocked her."

That was a shocker. "Am I a suspect? Should I have a lawyer?" I asked.

"Let's say you *could* be a suspect very easily. And if you want a lawyer, you're free to park your ass in here until one shows up"

Now I was steamed. My ire got the better of me and I shot back, "Bullshit! I'm not under arrest, I can walk out of here if I want to. If you thought you had anything on me, you'd have arrested me already."

The daggers in Detective Tosca's eyes were almost literal. I didn't like his flippant attitude, and I didn't want to let that accusation pass unanswered. At the same time, I didn't need to alienate a homicide detective. "Look *detective*," I continued, emphasizing the word "detective." "Megan was my friend and that's all. I liked her. I didn't have any reason to kill her. And if you ask around the office, you won't find anybody to even hint that we were ever romantically involved. Besides, up to Thursday, she had a boyfriend."

I probably should have stopped there, but I was rolling. Adrenaline kept pushing me along. "If you're at a loss for suspects, why don't you look at that asshole boyfriend of hers. He's a sketchy character. And according to what she told me the last day I saw her, he popped her one last Thursday night and she kicked him out. How's *that* for motive?"

"Are you telling *me* how to run *my* investigation?" Tosca barked.

"No, sir!" I shot back. Thinking: *Somebody should tell you.*

Detective Tosca glared at me for a full thirty seconds without saying a word. If the interview weren't being videoed, I expect he would have hauled out the rubber hoses. Finally, he fiddled with his notebook, then his scowl deepened, and he growled, "Where were *you* last Friday night?"

"After I dropped off Megan, who, by the way, was alive and well when I left her, I went home, walked the dog, ate a couple of hotdogs and read. And it may not be relevant, but after I left Megan's apartment Saturday, I spent evening drinking too many martinis and thinking about my wife."

"Where *is* your wife?"

"In the cemetery. She died four years ago, traffic accident."

"What happened to her?" he asked. Insensitively put, but I thought maybe I heard a soupçon of sympathy in the question.

"Guy on a motorcycle flying down Grant Street at 80 blew through a red light and hit her. He wiped out and died, too. Coroner determined he was high on cocaine. It wouldn't have mattered if he were Mother Theresa, though, my wife was still dead."

Tosca scribbled, then moved the questioning back to the present. "Is there anybody who can vouch for your whereabouts Friday night?"

"Only my dog, Champ."

"Not much of an alibi witness." Tosca observed

"No, I guess not. But as I pointed out the other day, If I'd known I was going to need an alibi, I'd have been more careful about constructing one."

"Nobody at Press Grill remembered you being there Saturday, either."

"Wonderful. But I do have the charge slip."

Tosca raised an eyebrow and changed the subject. "How come it was you that found the body?"

"She told me about the boyfriend hitting her when I drove us home from work Friday. I worried that he might come back and really do a number on her. I called her a couple of times and she didn't answer. I texted her, too, but she didn't answer those either. I got worried and decided to check on her."

"You didn't leave messages when you called." A statement, not a question.

"No, Megan never listened to her voice mail. People who knew her didn't bother to leave messages."

"How did you get in her apartment? You got a key?" There was that accusing tone again.

"No, detective, I didn't have a key. I slipped through the outer door when a group of people came out. Megan's door was pulled to but not latched. I called out to her and got no answer. Then I pushed open the door, stepped inside, and found what I found."

"How'd you know which apartment was hers? The building doesn't have a directory."

"I'd been up to her place one, two, maybe three times in the couple of years that we've known each other."

More scribbling. "Touch anything when you got in?"

"Nothing that I recall. I used my jacket sleeve on the edge of the door handle so I wouldn't leave prints or disturb any that were there."

I thought that latter comment might kick loose a word of thanks, but it didn't.

"I'll have a statement for you to sign before you go," Tosca announced. "Wait here."

I didn't ask how long I was supposed to wait since he probably wouldn't have told me, and it wouldn't matter anyway. I checked my phone for email and played some frames of Angry Birds before Tosca came back into the room with Vickers not far behind. About an hour had passed.

"This is your statement," Vickers said, as she dropped a couple of sheets of paper in front of me. "Read it carefully and, if you agree with it, sign it. If not, tell us how you want it changed."

Someone had taken Tosca's questions and my answers and rather skillfully stitched them in to a concise but comprehensive narrative of my activities from the time I dropped Megan off Friday afternoon to the time I discovered her battered and lifeless body on Saturday. It seemed accurate enough so far as I could tell, so I signed the last page and handed it back to Detective Vickers.

"May I have a copy," I asked?

She nodded silently and left the room, returning shortly with a Xerox copy of the statement, which she handed to me. "You're free to go," she said.

"For now," Tosca added balefully.

Not wishing to prolong such a delightful experience, I mumbled some goodbyes, and stood to go.

"Don't leave town, West," Tosca barked when I got to the door. How cinematic, I thought to myself, but said nothing, deciding that a snappy retort would not be in my best interest. As quickly as possible, I left the interview room and headed for the building exit. I smiled and gave a little wave goodbye to the Hispanic officer at the desk as I walked out. She smiled and waved back.

CHAPTER 6

Tuesday morning, I thought to look for Megan's obituary. From the obituary page of the Columbus *Dispatch* website:

Megan Annette Simmons, age 22, of Columbus passed away Friday. She was born November 4, 1997 and raised in Westerville. She attended Westerville South High School (Class of 2014) and Columbus State Community College (Class of 2016). She is survived by her loving brother, Carl Simmons, 30, of Dublin. She was employed as a Systems Administrator by Comprehensive Information Systems in Columbus. Friends may call...

Another paragraph noted that funeral services would be Thursday at one of the prominent funeral homes in northeast Columbus. Looking at it again, I decided the obit was extremely slender, especially knowing how outgoing Megan was. There was no mention of activities, clubs, or volunteer work although I felt certain she had belonged to at least a couple of groups and volunteered regularly with some charities. The most shocking omission was any mention of her parents. I was fairly sure they still lived in Westerville but as far as the obit was concerned, they might never have existed. Strange. Could this be a clue to the whole nasty business?

By now, I had had to phone Brad and ask for more time. I needed the week off and that would be a hard, if not impossible, sell via email. Brad was understanding. He only had one concern. "Are you up to date on the ExGen project?" he asked.

"Yes," I replied, "I set up the test data before I left Friday." Thank goodness I stuck around and finished that copy, otherwise I'd be stuck with doing it this week. "And I don't think I have anything else due for them for at least a couple more weeks."

"Sounds good. Take the week." Brad offered his condolences and hung up.

Megan's case had dominated the local news since Saturday evening. Three days later, it was still the top story. From Channel 4, I learned that the police had not only questioned Megan's erstwhile boyfriend, Liam, but had taken him into custody. That was probably inevitable. He was a natural suspect because of his relationship with her. The fact that he had physically assaulted her right before her death put him squarely in the crosshairs of the police investigation. The newscast also reported that the coroner had determined that Megan died sometime Friday night, probably not too long after I dropped her off, and that death was due to blunt force trauma to the head. Despite being stripped nude and posed the way she was, the reporter said there was no indication of sexual assault.

I turned off the TV and pondered this new information for a while. Death by blunt force trauma was a foregone conclusion; I had seen Megan's body. It was a little surprising that there was no sexual assault, though. A nude body and suggestive posing typically indicate a sexual motivation, but that might be what the killer *wanted* everyone to think. As for the boyfriend, Liam Murphy was a foul ball for sure, barely able to hold on to his job as a cable

TV installer. He also had a temper as I well knew from observing it firsthand a time or two in the past. But despite the points against him, he was more of an ignorant rube than a psychopath. Try as I might, I just couldn't picture Liam Murphy as *vicious*. And Megan's attacker had been vicious.

I wondered if the police had surveillance video of the apartment building. You can't swing a dead cat these days without hitting a surveillance camera. If they had video, and if the video was of good enough quality, the cops might be able to identify the perp from it. Maybe that's why they arrested Liam, although I still had my doubts on that score.

I wanted to get back into my reading routine and, with all day free, it would have been the perfect opportunity to do just that. But the events of the week had so jangled my brain that I didn't think I could concentrate on anything weightier than the Sunday funny papers. So, I spent the day watching old *Star Trek* reruns. I lost myself in Kirk's and Spock's many adventures and still marveled at how Kirk always wound up with the prettiest woman in the episode.

I hadn't seen my neighbor, Jenna for a couple of days. That wasn't unusual. Sometimes I'd see her for several days in a row, then not for another week or two. Even though we lived on the same floor, our schedules didn't mesh well. She pulled three twelves—three twelve-hour shifts—at the hospital Wednesday, Thursday, and Friday, so I didn't expect to see her until maybe the weekend. But I found a note from her taped to my door when I came back in from walking Champ.

> Greg,
>
> Why don't you come by Friday evening? I want to make sure you are okay, and I suspect you could use some

company. I get off at 7:00. How about
8:30?

Jenna

I smiled. The note warmed me inside because I did enjoy
Jenna's company. She was pretty, vivacious, and easy to talk
to. Being with her was as comfortable as wearing a favorite
old jacket, although she probably wouldn't be thrilled at me
comparing her with outerwear. There was too large a gap in
our ages for there to be anything other than friendship, but I
still felt that spending Friday evening with her would be
preferable to sitting at home alone again. And at any rate, a
visit with her might be the tonic I needed to help me get over
this disastrous week.

I penned an enthusiastic "Yes!" at the bottom of the note
and slipped it under her door.

CHAPTER 7

Every funeral I have been to has been depressing. Megan's was no exception, especially since this was the first funeral I'd attended since Lisa's four years ago.

There was a lovely framed color portrait of Megan on the casket, closed, of course, due to the extent of her facial injuries. The photograph was so lifelike that I swear her green eyes sparkled out from the photo paper, setting off her titian hair perfectly. Had the picture come to life, I would have been only mildly surprised.

The flowers must have put at least a couple of florists in the black for the month. There were arrangements on stands and in vases, live plants in pots and cut flowers of every color and description. I recognized roses, hydrangeas, miniature sunflowers, daisies, and the inevitable peace lilies. There were many more that I couldn't identify. It was a riot of color and bloom types that Megan would have thoroughly enjoyed. Yet no amount of floral beauty could compensate for the fact that this bright, happy, lovable young woman was gone.

Most of the expected cast of characters was there. Megan's brother, Carl, was the chief mourner. There was a large contingent from CIS. Rob Ford was there, along with Henry Ames. So was Dexter Hackshaw, another member of my team, and Megan's boss whose name I didn't remember. My boss, Brad, was there. Even Judson Battenslag himself, the V.P., along with his wife, Cindy, had shown up. Conspicuous by their absence where the parental units, Mr. & Mrs. Simmons. I tucked this oddity away in the back of my brain, deciding it might deserve further investigation if the occasion arose. There was no sign of Liam Murphy, either, although he might still be a guest of the County and unable to attend. I wasn't sure if he had bonded out or not, or if the court had admitted him to bail.

The room was standard funeral parlor. The casket rested on a catafalque at one end, surrounded by the flowers sent by friends, extended family, and coworkers. Urns with large, frondy plants formed a palace guard at regular intervals against both the room's longer walls. Rows of chairs had been set up a discreet distance from the catafalque. A lectern stood, a lonely sentinel, beside the casket. The one unique note was the music. Instead of the usual dreary organ music emanating from hidden speakers, a string quartet comprised solely of women played upbeat classical music. The two violin players were young, the cellist was probably at least a decade older than me, while the woman with the viola was somewhere in between. "Kudos to Carl," I though, as the musicians evoked a happier mood than recordings of syrupy organ music.

The minister, I discovered from reading the program, was the pastor of a small nondenominational church over on Neil Avenue somewhere between Victorian Village and Harrison West. Apparently, Megan had attended regularly, something I did not know, and I thought it a bit odd that this fact had not made it into her brief obituary. Maybe Carl didn't know, or maybe it slipped his mind. From experience, I knew how stressful planning an unexpected funeral can be, and Megan was his baby sister.

I took my place in the line of people filing by to console the bereaved brother. When it was my turn, I said to him, "Carl, you haven't met me, but I'm Greg West. I worked with Megan and we carpooled to work. She was a very dear person, and I am terribly, terribly sorry for your loss."

Carl's voice was restrained, obviously choking back a flood of emotion, as he responded, "Ah, yes, Greg. Megan mentioned you to me on many occasions. Thank you so much for coming."

"I wouldn't—couldn't—not come," I replied.

The service itself consisted of a small procession of friends and coworkers stepping up to the lectern and sharing their memories of Megan. Tears in copious supply mixed with laughter as each person related a special story or memory, some funny, some sad to the other mourners. A goodly number of the speakers were women, although there were more than a few men as well, and their tears flowed almost as freely as the women's.

After the last speaker sat down, the minister rose to conduct the funeral service proper. Although I remember thinking at the time that it was a beautiful service, later I couldn't recall a single word he said before the final, "Amen!" Frankly, I was doing damned good to get through the thing without turning into a puddle of goo, so not remembering the sermon didn't seem like such a big deal.

As I was leaving, Rob, Henry, and Dex caught up with me. I was surprised to see all three of them wearing suits and ties, which was a radical departure from their attire in the office.

Rob was the first to accost me. "Greg! Were you really the one that found her?"

I replied, simply, "Yes."

Henry looked down and traced a design on the floor with the toe of his shoe. "Must've been awful," he said.

"Jesus Christ!" Dex exclaimed. "I'd've shit bricks!" The tip of his necktie bobbed up and down with agitation or excitement or both as he spoke.

"Well," I said, "it wasn't a picnic in the park, believe me!"

Rob looked around, then said in a low voice, "Hey, you know, something? I heard she reported old Battenslag to H.R. for sexual harassment. Think *he* offed her?"

Henry piped up, "Sure, he could have."

I chewed on that for a moment. Judson Foster Battenslag was a big, powerful man, and rumor had it that his and Cindy's marriage might be on the rocks. But Battenslag is the consummate corporate ladder-climber. I just couldn't see him risking his precious career to proposition a junior member of the technical staff. Still, it might merit consideration. However, I answered Rob and Henry with, "Doubtful. Jud Battenslag may be a horny old goat but he's not a *stupid* horny old goat."

We all laughed at that and headed out of the funeral home. Rob was obviously uncomfortable in a suit since he clawed off his tie before we got out the door.

On the drive home, I had several things to think over. One was the missing parents. Why were they not mentioned in the obituary and why had they skipped their only daughter's funeral? Another was Liam Murphy. Sure, he was a loser, but was he a cruel and violent loser? Maybe he was, but I wasn't so sure.

Finally, there was that tidbit about Jud Battenslag. I could see him romancing someone in the executive suite who might be useful in propelling his career forward, but would he really put the moves on a junior staffer to the point where she reported him to H.R., and then kill her for it? It sounded fantastic, but I admitted it was difficult to completely dismiss the possibility out of hand.

As I parked the Mustang in the garage and rode up to the tenth floor, I decided that it would be best to let the police do their job and catch the killer while I concentrated on getting mentally prepared to go back to work and do *my* job next week. A nagging voice in the back of my head told me that probably wasn't going to happen. I opened the door and Champ stood there with a doggy grin on his face, the helicopter rotating as furiously as ever.

CHAPTER 8

Friday dawned gloomy and cold again. Champ wasn't interested in spending any more time outside than necessary, so we skipped the dog park and camped in the condo most of the day. Early in the afternoon, I decided that what I needed to elevate my mood was a little kick-ass music. My entire music collection consists of MP3 files on my computer, which makes it very portable. I picked out some selections and cranked up the volume as I rocked out to the Rolling Stones. Mick and the boys had just finished *Hang Fire* and were crushing *Factory Girl*, the live version on *Flashpoint*, when Champ let out one of his infrequent barks, a single, insistent, "Woof!"

Champ apparently disapproves of my musical taste because every time I turn on the tunes, he retreats to another room. But the woof meant he heard someone at the door. I paused my private Stones concert and went to answer it. It was Tillie, my downstairs neighbor.

Tillie Truax lives on the ninth floor below me. She is of uncertain age and could be anywhere between twenty and fifty. She had lived in the building forever, at least since condo renovation. Her hair was jet black and of such a deep, even shade that it suggested regular applications of Miss Clairol. Today she had styled it, if you can call it styling, by heaping it on top of her head, somewhat like those Edwardian hairstyles you see on pictures of women from the early 1900s. Her speech has a breezy, breathy quality reminiscent of Jackie Kennedy and her manner was always so earnest that I wanted to laugh but did not dare to for fear of hurting her feelings. Tillie was so likeable that no one *ever* wanted to hurt her feelings.

Before I could speak, Tillie opened the conversation. "*Oh*, Mr. West," she breathed, "I do *so* hope you could turn your music down. I worked *so* late last night, and I simply *must* get a nap this afternoon." The words floated into the room on butterfly wings.

"Why Tillie, I *do* apologize," I replied, slightly mocking her earnestness. "I thought you'd be at work today and I have no problem turning the music down. In fact, I'll turn it completely off." I had no idea what Tillie did for a living or why she might have had to work late, but I had expected her to be gone during the day because she usually is.

"Oh, *thank* you *ever* so much, Mr. West." I've known her for the nearly four years that I've lived in the building, but Tillie still insists on calling me "Mr. West." I've been called worse.

"That was just *dreadful* about you finding that woman. It must have been a *terrible* shock. Are *you* okay? Do you *need* anything?"

Maybe the loud music was just an excuse to check on me, although I had been jamming. "Yes, Tillie, it was a real shock. Going to the funeral yesterday didn't help. But I'm better today, I promise, and I don't need anything at all."

"I'm *so* glad to hear that. That nice Miss Stone that lives down the hall said *she* was going to check up on you, *too*."

Tillie's earnestness was almost comical. Sweet Tillie. I said, "Yes, Jenna invited me to stop down this evening. I reckon everybody in the building is worried about me. It's flattering, but I really think I'll be fine."

"Well," she said, "*thank* you so *very much* for turning down the music. And you let me know if you need *anything*."

"You're welcome, Tillie. No problem."

I went back inside and closed the door. With Tillie departed for an afternoon siesta and my music muted, I decided to tackle reading again. I selected A. J. Baime's *The Accidental President*, an analysis of Harry Truman's first four months in office and the impact of those four months on subsequent world history. I read quietly until nearly eight. Then I snapped the leash on Champ's collar and took him out for his last walk of the evening.

Champ decided he wanted to walk up Spring Street. His rotating tail told of his excitement at being outdoors with his human. Once we got to Grant, we turned south to Gay Street, at Gay, we went west toward High, and finally back north. I kept an eye on the time, but Champ wasn't in the mood to dawdle today, so I had almost ten minutes to spare by the time we reached our building.

Back in the condo, I checked myself in the mirror. My shirt looked tired and wrinkled, so I washed my face and put on a clean one. Then I selected a bottle of Côtes du Rhône from my modest wine collection. I like good wine, but I find that modestly priced wines are usually every bit as enjoyable as the über-expensive ones, maybe except for Veuve Clicquot champagne. And while I enjoy many quite fine California wines, a French Côtes du Rhône is a nice touch for special occasions. This was a special occasion.

I pocketed my bottle opener, turned out the lights, walked out the door and down the hall toward Jenna's.

CHAPTER 9

Jenna greeted me at the door enveloped in an oversized snow-white terrycloth bathrobe. She wore no makeup, but I thought she looked fine without any. A few crinkles at the corners of her eyes added character to her face. Her honey blonde hair stood out against the stark white of the robe. Her teeth were almost as white as the robe and evenly spaced, except for a slight extra space between her two front incisors.

"Oh, am I too early?" I asked.

"No, I just wanted to be cozy tonight. Please, come on in. Oh, I see you brought wine. Let me take care of that for you." She fetched a decanter and two large wineglasses from her wine rack and placed them on the coffee table.

Jenna had arranged her living space such that two armchairs faced the coffee table, but at an angle, so two people could use the chairs and still have a conversation. A smallish sofa stood on the other side of the table. The furniture was all in earth tones that went well with the champagne colored carpet.

I uncorked the bottle and poured it into the decanter. "We'll let it breath a while," I said, and sat down in the chair on the right. Jenna took the other chair.

"Greg, I can't even begin to imagine the week you've had. How're you doing?"

"It's been a hell of a week," I admitted. "Finding Megan was shock enough, but then I had to deal with that crabby detective, and the funeral on top of that. I think the funeral was the worst. Everything about it reminded me of Lisa's. This whole week has royally sucked."

"The news, *all* the TV stations, had a pretty complete account of the crime scene and what happened when you found her. That had to be awful! What happened with the police?" She looked at me and I saw sympathy in her gray-blue eyes.

"There were two detectives, a woman and a man. I think the woman had more experience since she was older and seemed to be in charge. I talked to both of them briefly at the scene but the man, Detective Tosca, conducted the interview at headquarters. He wasn't any too cordial, either. I presumed they had a camera somewhere recording the performance and that Ms. Detective Vickers was watching a TV monitor in another room.

"Tosca tried to float the idea that *I* had killed Megan because she'd rebuffed a sexual advance, but that never happened. Not only was she decades younger than me, but she also had a boyfriend. And from what I gathered from our commuting conversations, she had a talent for picking losers, somebody my Dad would have called a bum magnet."

Gray-blue eyes studied me carefully. It would be easy to lose myself in those eyes.

"The other problem I had with the interview is that I couldn't account for my time Friday night or Saturday morning. That is, I could account for it but not prove it. Friday night, I stayed in. I *did* go out for lunch Saturday but according to the detective, nobody at the restaurant remembered me being there. If dogs could testify, Champ could alibi me for Friday, but they can't, and right now I'm up that proverbial stinky creek with no visible means of propulsion.

Jenna smiled, and her eyes danced with humor. I noticed how their gray-blue hue perfectly complemented the honey blonde hair that caressed her shoulders. "The thought of your dog testifying, you know, on the witness stand in court," she said, "strikes me funny."

I poured some of the Côtes du Rhône into each of the glasses. We clinked them, and Jenna said, "To better days ahead."

"To seeing this shit in the rearview." I said. We each took a sip. I had to admit to myself that this was an exceptionally good wine, and not a budget-buster, either.

I continued my report of Detective Tosca's grilling. "When I suggested to Tosca that the cops might want to look at the boyfriend, he got his boxers in a bunch. But I guess they did arrest him. Did you know that he and Megan had a fight that turned physical just the day before she was killed?"

"No," Jenna replied slowly, "I did not. But I heard on TV that they let the boyfriend go yesterday evening."

That surprised me. "Let him go! You mean they released him, or did he bond out?"

"They let him go. Said they didn't have enough evidence to hold him, at least that's what they said on TV. It was some black woman from the police."

"Sounds like Detective Vickers," I said. "I'm confident she's the brains of that team, so if *she* turned Liam Murphy loose, there must have been a good reason. At least I hope that's the case."

Jenna's face brightened. "That's right, I remember now. The titles on the screen said, 'Detective Sharona Vickers.'" She picked up her wineglass and took another sip. I did the same, except my sip wasn't quite as dainty.

"You know," I mused, "I'm a little puzzled now. I figured Murphy would be the odds-on favorite suspect. But then after the funeral, I heard a rumor that she'd reported old Battenslag to Human Resources for making improper advances to her. One of the guys at the office thought *he* might have been involved."

"Batten who?" Jenna asked. As a cardiac care nurse, she had only a vague idea of what I did and, of course, knew virtually nothing about the people at CIS.

"Judson Battenslag. He's a bigwig V.P. at CIS. Frankly, I'd be inclined to discount that story. Battenslag is a climber. He might have tried to romance her if she'd been somebody in a position to help advance his career, but I seriously doubt he'd risk shagging the help, so to speak. You never really know, though."

Jenna thought that over. "You got any other ideas?"

I considered that for a moment, then slowly answered, "It's not so much an idea as a curiosity. You didn't go to the funeral so you wouldn't have noticed this, but the only family member there was her brother, Carl. No sign of the parents, and I'm reasonably sure they're still living. The obituary didn't mention them, either. By the way, that obituary was really sparse, more so than most of the obits I've seen. It didn't contain much beyond the barest of facts. I don't know exactly what any of it means, but something's screwy."

I poured more wine and let that last tidbit hang in the air.

Jenna looked thoughtful for a moment. "Yes," she agreed, "I'd say that's strange. I mean, even if the parents were dead, the obit should have said 'Preceded in death by' or something like that."

I agreed and sipped some more of my wine while Jenna did the same. We sat silently for a few moments. Then she gently said, "I know this is kind of personal, but do you think you need to see somebody, like a counselor or something?"

"I don't know, maybe, but right now I'm concentrating on getting my act together to go back to work next week."

More silence. I refilled our glasses with the last of the Côtes du Rhône. Then Jenna spoke. "I never lost anybody, to death, I mean, so it's a little difficult to fully comprehend what you're dealing with and going through. The only one I ever lost was Ben and I was so angry with *him* that I'd've shot him out of a cannon to get rid of him."

"Ben" would be Benton Diehl, Jenna's ex-husband. "I knew you were divorced, but I don't know any of the details. It doesn't sound like it was amicable."

"Amicable!" she laughed. "It was about as opposite from amicable as you can get. Think Hatfields and McCoys." She drank the last of her wine, leaned back in the chair, took a deep breath, and started telling me about her divorce. "Benton Diehl was a charming douchebag. I met him when I was in nursing school. I was only nineteen and, while I wasn't exactly naïve, I hadn't seen much of the world beyond Keene, New Hampshire. He was older and seemed to me to be the most sophisticated man in the world. We got married.

"I thought I was happily married, at least for the first few years. I went to graduate school, got my MSN, and went to work for a hospital in Portland, Maine. What I *didn't* know, and only found out fifteen years later, was that Ben also had a girlfriend. He was seeing her when he met me, and he continued to see her all the while we were married."

"Jeez! What an asshole!" *Sympathy is cold comfort*, I thought.

"Yeah, we'd been married fifteen years when he accidentally left his cell phone at home one day. I happened to see a text from a woman that was very, very, shall we say, personal. When I confronted him, he admitted the whole thing. I told him to get the hell out and I haven't seen him since. The lawyers handled the divorce, and I didn't have to go to court at all."

"He must have *wanted* you to find out, if he left his unlocked phone out for you to find it," I mused.

"I don't know, maybe," she replied, "but not necessarily. You see, he'd set the phone so that our apartment was one of those trusted places where it unlocked automatically."

"I hope you got a good settlement."

She laughed without mirth. "Ha! I got squat!" She almost spat the words. "Ben never made much money and spent most of what he did make. I made more than he did, and we didn't have that many assets to split. Hell, I'm lucky I didn't have to pay *him* alimony."

"You're Jenna Stone, not Jenna Diehl. You must've taken your name back."

"That's about all there was *to* take back. It was a pain in the ass to change everything back, even more than changing it when I got married in the first place. But I didn't want anything else to do with Benton Diehl and I *certainly* didn't want his name."

"How long ago was all this?"

"Just before I moved here. When the divorce was final, I got this job here in Columbus and bought this condo."

"Wow." It was kind of nonsensical reply, but I couldn't think of anything weighty to say. Then I added, "You seem to be in a better place now."

"Yes, I'm successful in my career. I have a good job, make decent money, and I like living here."

We sat for a while in silence. Oddly, it wasn't awkward. Finally, I stood up to go and said, "I know you pulled a twelve today. I'll bet you're exhausted after working twelve straight hours. It felt good to talk this over, but I'm sorry I dredged up you divorce story."

"Ancient history," she smiled. "Dead, buried, and mostly forgotten." She had a captivating smile.

"Thanks for having me over."

She stood when I did. I realized almost for the first time that she was very tall for a woman, only a couple of inches or so shorter than me, in her bare feet. When she reached up, took my face in both her hands, and pulled me toward her to kiss me, I hardly had to bend over at all.

I expected a simple goodnight buss, but this kiss was long, tender, and deep. I didn't resist.

Before I knew what was happening, she had slipped the bathrobe off and let it drop to the floor. She stood naked before me, which left me momentarily stunned. Then I realized I was staring at her. Manners and modesty told me to avert my gaze, but my eyes simply refused to look away. I knew she was about forty, plus or minus, but her body, trim and firm, looked at least a decade younger. I sensed that she welcomed the appraisal.

An impish grin danced at the corners of Jenna's mouth. She took my right hand in her left and silently led me into her bedroom.

CHAPTER 10

After we made love, we lay in bed loosely entwined, silently enjoying the closeness of each other. I was about to drift off to sleep when Jenna whispered, "You know, I was afraid when I dropped the bathrobe, you'd bolt out the door."

"A lot of things ran through my mind," I murmured in reply. "But I guarantee you that bolting was not one of them." Then I slipped off to dreamland.

I woke somewhere around midnight. Jenna's soft breathing told me she was asleep. Gently, I disentangled myself and sat up on the edge of the bed. A vortex of thoughts and emotions whirled through my head.

I wasn't about to complain, but I didn't see what attracted Jenna to *me*. She's a charming woman in the prime of life and I'm almost—not quite—a senior citizen. I'm not the elephant man, but I'm not going to win any beauty contests either. Women had never chased me or come on to me. That Jenna had done so perplexed me. I can't say that it displeased me, though.

There was also a tinge of guilt. Did being with Jenna make me disloyal to Lisa? The marriage vows say, "until death do us part," but I had a difficult time shaking the feeling that sleeping with another woman was a betrayal of my dead wife. It had been a lonely four years since I lost Lisa. Being with a woman again made me realize how much I missed the intimacy. Part of me was craving the close connection with another human being. Sex was part of it, but it was more than just sex. I ended up thinking that Lisa might approve. Since she couldn't be here herself, she would want me to find someone to be happy with, wouldn't she? I hoped she would.

Jenna stirred slightly, turned over, and resumed her regular breathing.

I wondered what was going in *her* mind. What would she be thinking in the morning? Was this an impulse at the spur of the moment? Had she planned this as a one-night stand? That would be awkward, since we both lived in the same building, on the same floor, even. Did she want to be friends with benefits, maybe? Or was she as eager for a real relationship as I was? Those questions needed answers, but, obviously, no answers would be forthcoming tonight.

I thought about the age difference again and its implications for a long-term relationship. I wasn't sure exactly how old Jenna was. My best estimate based on hints I'd picked up talking to her was that she was in her early forties, or perhaps her late thirties. I was at least a decade and a half older, potentially a huge difference a few years from now. Would she really want to tie herself in to a man who might need a nursing home while she still had plenty of life to live? Longevity and health are difficult to predict, but if I turned into a doddering old man while she was just entering her so-called "golden years," how would she react?

Realizing that I wasn't going to get any answers tonight, I lay back down, pulled the covers up, and slowly, inexorably drifted back to sleep.

Bells started ringing and wouldn't stop, rousing me out of a deep sleep. I sensed it was morning and eventually understood that the bells were the ringtone on Jenna's phone and that is what had interrupted my slumber. Jenna was lying on her side with her back turned. I heard her softly talking but the sound was so muffled I couldn't make out the words until she concluded the call with, "Okay, I'll be there. Bye."

She turned toward me and said, "That was the hospital. They want me to cover for a nurse who called off. I'd hoped this wouldn't happen, but I *am* on call this weekend."

"I'm sorry you have to go." My disappointment must have been more obvious than I'd intended.

"Yes, I'm sorry, too, but this *is* my on-call weekend." Disappointment was evident in her voice as well when she said, "I had very different plans for *this* Saturday."

She and me both. "About last night…" I started.

She placed a forefinger to my lips and said, "Not now. Later. Gotta run. I have to be on the floor in less than an hour."

The kiss she gave me before dashing off toward the shower was luscious. I told her I'd see her later and walked slowly down the hall to my own unit. Champ's helicopter tail rotated vigorously at full velocity when I opened the door.

"Champ, old boy, not going to believe what happened to me last night." I didn't bother to regale my dog with the tale of my encounter with Jenna, but I think he understood that something special had happened anyway. I was on top of the world this morning, and Champ acted as if he were sitting right there on top with me.

CHAPTER 11

To my disappointment, and, hopefully, to Jenna's as well, the hospital called her in again Sunday. That meant I would have to brace myself for my return to the office the following day alone. Champ and I took advantage of the improved weather to spend Sunday afternoon walking all the way down to Schiller Park in German Village. I thought about finding a clock and taking a selfie in front of it holding up Sunday's newspaper but dismissed the idea as paranoid. Besides, with the ubiquity of mobile phones, there aren't too many clocks in public places anymore.

There is no way anyone, especially a person living alone, can alibi *all* his time. I decided not to let Detective Tosca get under my skin and concentrated on enjoying the day. Champ appeared to be enjoying it for he had the helicopter rotor going in full motion.

Monday's weather matched my mood. The thermometer had dropped into the mid-thirties and dull gray altostratus clouds scudded across the sky, mostly blocking the sun. Driving to work without Megan was eerie and I pressed the accelerator as much as I dared, just to get it over with.

My hopes of getting together with Jenna after her Sunday shift didn't pan out. I talked to her briefly, but she said she was exhausted after the weekend and was going straight to bed. I hoped this wasn't an excuse to avoid me, but she sounded completely spent so I decided she was telling the literal truth. I should probably stop overthinking these things, but sometimes I can't help myself.

Rob and Dexter materialized at my cubicle almost as soon as I sat down, and Henry wasn't far behind. Rob spoke in an excited whisper. "Did you hear? The cops were in old man Battenslag's office first thing this morning. One was a tall Italian-looking dude and the other was a short, chubby Black chick."

Tosca and Vickers.

"I heard he was boning Megan and she threatened to tell that wife of his," Dex whispered conspiratorially. I found that accusation hard to swallow. First, I didn't see Megan having sex with Battenslag. And if she *were* doing it with him, I felt I knew her well enough to be pretty sure that she wouldn't kiss and tell.

Rob chimed in, "Then there's that H.R. thing *I* heard about."

I waited for Henry to add something, but when he didn't, I decided to weigh in myself. "Guys," I said evenly, "both of those ideas seem pretty far-fetched to me. I think I knew Megan well enough to say she probably wasn't boinking Battenslag, and even if she was, she wouldn't have ratted him out."

Looking up, I saw Vickers and Tosca heading in my direction. Their faces clearly said, "We're on a mission. "Christ!" I exclaimed to the guys, but not loud enough, I hoped, for the two detectives to hear. "This day was already shitty enough and now it's heading straight down the dumper."

"We want to talk to *you*." Tosca was his usual charming self, displaying what was apparently his entire complement of social graces.

"I'm not in much of a talking mood today," I replied. And I meant it.

Detective Vickers now took the conversational lead. "Mr. West," she began, I'm sorry to bother you here at work, but we thought you might be able to give us a little more background on the victim, ah, Megan. Is there somewhere we could talk privately?" She shot a dark look at the trio of Dex, Rob, and Henry hovering around my cubicle.

I responded better to her gentler approach. "Yes, there's a conference room around the corner that I think is vacant now."

I lead the way. CIS has all kinds of conference rooms. Some are large, some are small. Some have extensive audio-visual setups, some are spartan. The room I selected was one of the latter. It contained a small, rectangular table with two slightly uncomfortable-looking chairs on each side and one at each end. I sat down nearest the door in case I decided to make a hasty exit. The two detectives sat across from me, Vickers facing me on my left and Tosca facing me to the right.

"Mr. West," Detective Vickers began, "I want to apologize again for disturbing you at your office. I understand this is your first day back at work since the tragedy. But I'm—we're—hoping you can help us understand more about Miss Simmons."

I noticed she again referred to Megan by name, not as "the victim." Nice touch.

Vickers continued, "We feel that our investigation would be moved along considerably if we knew more about her, what kind of person she was, who her friends were, and things like that. Do you think you can help?"

I thought for a minute. As well as I felt I had known Megan, I realized I didn't know very much about her friends.

Finally, I said, "I'll try. Truth is, although I learned a lot about Megan as a person carpooling with her, I don't really know much about who she ran with. You might start with the brother, Carl."

"Yes," she said, "he's on our list, but we haven't run him down yet."

"And I presume you talked with the boyfriend, or ex-boyfriend, I guess he was." Since Megan had kicked him out the day before her death, that made him an ex in my book.

"Yeah, of course." That was Tosca's contribution. He was oddly restrained today. Vickers must have clamped a lid on him.

"We did talk with Mr. Murphy," Vickers added. "We talked with him quite a bit, and we did get some information from him."

"Have you talked to her coworkers in Desktop Support?" I asked.

"Mr. Battenslag suggested that," she replied. We're seeing them next."

"Megan was a sweet girl with a sunny outlook on life," I stated. "She seemed to have a talent for picking loser boyfriends, but other than that, I wouldn't consider that she lived a high-risk lifestyle. Everybody seemed to like her.

"There is one thing that puzzled me, though. I'd swear that her parents are still living, but they were not at the funeral and there was not a word about them in the obituary. Maybe the brother knows something about that"

Vickers glanced at Tosca who scribbled something in his notebook.

"Other than that," I continued, "I'm not sure that I have anything substantial to add."

Sensing that they had gathered all they were going to get, Vickers rose, and Tosca followed suit. "Thank you so much for your time," she said. "And again, we're sorry for having to disturb you on such a difficult day."

Her words sounded genuine and I believe she was genuinely sorry. A glance at Tosca's face told me that he wasn't sorry a bit.

CHAPTER 12

I sat in a booth at Chile Verde Café munching chips and salsa and watching the customers come in. An attractive young woman came through the door, saw me, smiled, and then walked over and sat down in my booth.

"Hello, Daddy," she said.

Heather always called me Daddy. She was my baby and I loved it. My "baby" was now 24 years old, close to Megan's age, I realized. She was almost a carbon copy of her mother except her hair was light brown instead of Lisa's dark brunette and she had hazel eyes. She had the same petite build that Lisa had when we married, along with her mother's smile and dimples.

"I heard you found that woman's body," she said, visibly shuddering. "How awful!"

"It was."

"Do you want to talk about it?"

"No."

At this point, the server rescued me by coming to take our order. Heather ordered a taco salad while I went with the tamales. Since Chile Verde serves only Pepsi and not Coke products, I ordered an iced tea to drink.

Heather gave me a long, appraising look after the server left. "Daddy, there's something different about you." A pause, then "Are you sleeping with somebody?"

Unlike many children who don't want to—or can't— think about their parents as sexual beings, Heather had always felt free to discuss sex and sexuality with me.

Consequently, I had little trouble reciprocating. "Yes," I responded, "I am. At least I did. I'm not sure where it's going, though."

Heather's interest perked up. "Tell me about her."

"Her name is Jenna, she's a nurse in the cardiac care unit at St. Agatha. She has a condo on my floor and she's younger than I am."

"How young?" I had hoped to gloss over the age difference, but Heather jumped on it like a dog on a bone.

"I'm not sure, exactly. I think she's fortyish."

Heather relaxed a bit, probably relieved that I wasn't seeing someone in her own age group. "That's not *too* much difference,"

"It's not now; I'm worried it might be down the road."

"Daddy, none of us knows how far that road goes. Look at that poor woman you carpooled with. *She* ended up murdered and never made it past her twenties. Take care of the now and let 'down the road' take care of itself." Wise girl. "Tell me more about this Jenna person."

I told her that Jenna and I had got to know each other gradually since she moved in, mostly casual conversations but enough of them for us to become friends. Then I told her about Friday night.

"Holy cats!" Heather exclaimed. Then she giggled. After pausing to reflect a moment, she continued, "Jenna sounds like she's something else. Tell me more!"

"She's very tall for a woman, almost as tall as I am."

"Statuesque?"

"I suppose you could say that. She's tall and slender but not skinny, has honey blonde hair that falls enticingly over her shoulders, and her eyes are an interesting and riveting gray blue. And her smile is enchanting."

"You sound like you're in love!" she charged.

The arrival of our food provided a break from Heather's inquisition. But not for long.

"You really like her, don't you, Daddy? *Are* you in love with her?"

"I do. And I don't know."

"I want to meet her."

"I think you will—someday."

Heather gave a little frown before insisting, "Not someday. Soon."

"We'll see. I don't want to scare her off by pushing family at her."

"Daddy," she said, "if I'm reading the tea leaves right, she won't be scared off. I mean, *she* came on to *you!*"

I had to admit that this made sense.

"Honey, it's been so long since I dated that I'm not sure I even know how to go about it now."

Heather giggled again. "Sounds like you're doing just fine."

"The other thing is you know your Mom and I had a really terrific marriage. I guess in the back of my mind there's the thought that another relationship isn't going to measure up. Besides, I don't want to disrespect your mother's memory."

"Daddy," she said sternly, "you have a lot of life left to live. You don't have to do it alone. You know, Mom and I talked about love, too. She adored you, you know."

I nodded silently.

"Mom was happiest when you were happy. I believe she would want you to have a good woman in your life now. Maybe Jenna is the one. You think?"

"I don't know. Part of me would like to think so. Anyway, what about all this life I have left to live? I thought you said I couldn't count on 'down the road.'"

"You can't *count* on it, but you can't assume there *isn't* a future, either."

"You make a lot of sense, sweetie. I just have to wrap my mind around it."

"Oh, Daddy!" she said simply. Then, "I want to meet this lady friend of yours."

"Let's give it a little more time. I don't want to rush things."

"You *are* going to see her again, aren't you?"

"I plan to. The other night just, well, happened. We haven't even really talked about it. She got called into work the next morning and had to dash off before we had the chance to."

"You're overthinking this, Daddy. You're making it too complicated! She wants you—obviously—and I think *you* want *her*."

It may not be normal to get relationship advice from your daughter; parents are supposed to be the ones giving the advice. But I've learned that Heather often has more wisdom and insight into relationships than people much older than she is. She'd given me some things to think about, that's for sure.

I changed the subject. "How are you and Doug?" Doug Lewis is a young attorney at the Dublin law firm where Heather works as a paralegal. Her hazel eyes sparkled at the mention of his name.

"Doug and I are fine. He wants to take me to the art museum this weekend. We've both been too busy to have much 'together' time lately, so it'll make a nice date"

I smiled. If Heather asked for my approval to date Doug, which she *never* would, I would give it.

I slurped the last of my iced tea, a little more noisily than I meant to, then motioned the server for the check. "When you see him, give Doug a hello from your Dad."

"Sure. Will you do the same, I mean, give Jenna a hello from me?"

I smiled again. "Sure, honey."

I signed the credit card slip, gathered my card and receipts, and stood up to leave. Heather gave me a big hug and a peck on the check.

"Bye, Daddy. Thanks for lunch."

"You're welcome. We'll do it again soon."

She bounded out of the restaurant, a young woman with places to go, leaving me standing alone beside the booth.

CHAPTER 13

I hoped I could get through Tuesday without another visit from Detective Tosca. Vickers I could tolerate, but Tosca made my hair itch. I had barely bought my first Diet Coke of the day and sat down at my keyboard when Rob and Dex materialized outside my cubicle.

"Morning, guys," I muttered, hoping they'd catch the hint that I was busy. They didn't.

Rob was barely able to contain himself. "I hear Battenslag called off today," he said in his most gossipy tone. "*I* think the cops are interviewing him."

"Rob, you're a one-string banjo. Maybe the guy just wanted a day off, or maybe he's sick. You can't assume that because he's not here he's sparring with Tosca and Vickers."

Henry must have seen us talking, or else he sensed it, because he wandered over from InfoSec.

Rob continued, "But I told you what I heard about Megan—"

I cut him off. "Rob, the more I think about your idea the crazier it sounds."

Dexter chimed in. "I have to go with Greg on this one. Jud doesn't strike me as a guy who's going to boink girls from the office."

"Any guy," Rob replied earnestly, "could be boinking any girl."

Henry decided to join in. "*I* heard the old horndog is boinking half the chicks on the third floor, at least the ones under thirty."

It was time to end this pointless distraction. "Rob," I said, "and Henry, and you too, Dex, I have a fairly good idea Megan wasn't sleeping with *anybody* at CIS. She had a live-in boyfriend up to the day before she died and anybody who knew the boyfriend would think twice about trying to snake her away from *him*.

"Now, I have real work to do today and *this* is a distraction. Can we put this meaningless shit to bed?"

Dex grinned slightly as Rob slunk glumly back to his cube and Henry slithered back to InfoSec.

I *did* have real work to do. Over two thousand emails had piled up while I was out last week, and I needed to sort through them. The unimportant ones I could simply delete but some of them needed a response and a few required that I actually *do* something. I spent yesterday's lunch hour meeting Heather, and today I had plans for another long lunch that did not involve food. I intended to try to locate Megan's brother.

I put all thoughts of my noontime mission out of my head for now and concentrated on the batch of changes Brad had assigned to me. I was busily at work when my cell phone rang. I was almost pleased that it was a telemarketer instead of Detective Tosca.

Brad stopped by my desk midmorning to check up on me. I guess he expected me to crack up or melt down, but I assured him I was not likely to do either.

"Brad, I'm okay," I assured him.

Brad stroked his bald pate with his left hand. "You had a lot to deal with last week," he said, the concern evident in his voice.

"Yes, I did, but I'm not such a delicate flower that I can't handle it."

"Have you seen a therapist? You know that our insurance plans cover that."

"No, Brad. I'm talking things over with a close friend and that's helping. And yes, I am familiar with our mental health benefits. I promise, if I need someone like that, I'll go. But I don't think that will help me any right now."

"In a way I'm glad, because I have a lot of tasks that you're the best person for, but I don't want to push you over the edge."

"I'm not *on* the edge."

"Okay, then. *Please* let me know if that changes." He was almost begging.

"I will, Brad. I will."

With that, he strode off towards his own cubicle.

Plowing through the backlog of emails was bad enough without the steady arrival of new messages, each announced by the whang of my new mail sound effect. Whang! Someone on another team copied half the company explaining how he fixed something that had no bearing on what I do. Delete. Whang! Players wanted for the company volleyball team. Delete. Whang! Blood drive next month. Set a reminder to schedule an appointment. Whang! Congratulations on somebody in accounting's promotion. Delete. And so it went for the rest of the morning.

With all the new incoming mail, I was surprised to see myself making a visible dent in the backlog. If I kept this up, I'd be through all my unread messages before the end of the week. Assuming, of course, that the level of incoming messages was manageable, and that Rob, Dex, and Henry didn't interrupt me too often to offer more irrelevant theories about who was boinking whom in the office.

My progress put me in a reasonably good mood and fortified me for my lunchtime excursion. I locked my screens and headed for the car.

CHAPTER 14

I didn't have a number or address for Carl Simmons, but I knew he sold cars for one of the hoity-toity dealerships clustered around Avery Road in Dublin. Dublin and Citygate Drive are not exactly close to each other, but Megan's AWOL parents were really bugging me. I decided to make the drive to try to locate the elder Simmons sibling.

The official name for the outer belt around Columbus is the "Jack Nicklaus Freeway," in honor of one of Columbus's favorite native sons. The former golf pro also has a museum dedicated to him on the campus of his alma mater, The Ohio State University. But locals almost always call the beltway "270," after its numeric designation, Interstate 270. From my office to the Dublin dealerships is a good twenty-plus mile excursion. Fortunately, the traffic at lunch time is rather easily navigable, and in less than half an hour I had reached my goal. I found Carl Simmons at my second stop, the Land Rover dealership.

Simmons didn't seem to remember me, so I reintroduced myself. "My name is Greg West, Mr. Simmons. We met at Megan's funeral, but I'm sure you were too distracted to remember me. Megan and I worked at the same company and we carpooled to work together."

A faint glimmer of recognition flickered across his face. "Yeah, I remember she talked about carpooling with some dude, and I did see you at the funeral." The memory of Megan's funeral was obviously fresh, raw, and unpleasant. "How can I help you, Mr. West? You lookin' to buy a car? I can get you a sweet deal on a Rover."

I assured Carl that I was happy with my Mustang and not, in fact, looking for a car. "Actually, Mr. Simmons…"

"Call me Carl."

"Okay. Actually, Carl, I was hoping to get some personal information. I'd understand if you don't want to talk about this, but as Megan's friend, I'm curious." I subtly emphasized the word "friend,"

"Megan and I carpooled for almost two years, and I always had the impression that her—your—parents are still living. Yet the obituary didn't mention them, and they weren't at the funeral."

Simmons's expression darkened, but I soon realized his anger wasn't directed at me. "They disowned her," he spat.

"Disowned?"

"Yeah, cut off all contact. As far as they were concerned, for all intensive purposes, she died back then."

I ignored the urge to remind Carl that the phrase was "for all intents and purposes." I wanted information, not an angry car salesman.

Simmons continued, "You see, it started with that butterfly tattoo she got when she was sixteen." I remembered seeing the tattoo when I found poor Megan stretched out on her floor.

Simmons continued. "You're supposed to have a parent's permission to get a tattoo if you're under eighteen, but Megan found a tattoo artist that either didn't care or didn't check the paperwork too carefully. Mom came in her room one day while Megan was getting dressed, saw that tattoo, and freaked. I mean, it was pretty small, and it weren't tacky or nothing, but the 'rents threw a genuine hissy anyway. To their way of thinking, nice girls didn't get tattoos.

"Then when she was a senior, Megs told 'em she was moving in with her boyfriend. Mom and Dad really lost it and they had a hell of a fight. Told her that no daughter of theirs was going to live in sin—that's the way they put it—and if that's what she was going to do, she could get the hell out and never come back. Sure, the guy was a shitheel—Megs always seemed to end up with dim bulbs and doofuses—but she was my baby sister. *I* couldn't pretend she didn't exist, even if she did hit a foul ball now and then. Hell, mistakes and bad choices are part of life."

That stunned me. It was cold, even for the most strait-laced of parents. "So, they never saw her or talked to her after that?"

"No. They didn't answer her calls or return her messages. A couple times, she came to the house, and they wouldn't even open the door. Like she never existed. I thought it was creepy, myself."

No shit, I thought. Then to Carl, "So, that's why you didn't include them in the funeral?"

"Yeah, like I said, to them she died when she was seventeen."

"Do *you* still have contact with them?"

"Yeah," he said, "I mean they're still my parents. They knew I was in touch with Megs, but we never talked about it and they didn't want to hear nothing about her. She was off limits as a topic of conversation. It was kinda weird and all, but I was in a tough spot. I mean, Megs needed *some* family, and I was all she had."

"I understand. Then they had no idea where she was or what she was doing?"

"Naw."

"And you didn't tell them she'd been killed?"

"No. Like I said, she died to them when she was in high school. They probably heard about it on the news, but they never said a word."

"I'm terribly sorry," I said, and I was. "Did you know her latest boyfriend, Liam Murphy?"

"Met him once. Another loser far as I was concerned. I wish that for just once Megs had connected with a nice, decent guy, but, like I said, she had a talent for picking the duds."

"Besides pegging him for a loser, did you have any other impressions?"

Simmons thought for a minute, then said, "Yeah, he wasn't dumb, but he *was* ignorant. Just some rube. Like I said, I only met him once. Seemed to treat Megs okay, though. Least she never complained about him hitting her."

"He did hit her, once, the day before she died, and she threw him out."

"Yeah," Simmons nodded, "that would be Megs. She wouldn't stand for being anybody's punching bag."

"Thank you for your time, Carl, and for sharing what must be a very painful subject for you."

He looked down as he replied, "Aw, it's okay." Then he looked back up with an earnest face. "You know, I loved my kid sister and would have done anything for her, even if she did screw up now and then. It hurts she's gone."

As an afterthought, he posed a question, "Hey, you don't know anybody that wants a coupla cats, do you? I've got Megan's two cats, but I have to keep 'em in the basement 'cause my kid's allergic." Mimosa and Smoke needed a home.

"Maybe. I'm not sure. I'll let you know." Maybe Jenna liked cats.

I thanked him again, fired up the Mustang, and pointed it back toward the office.

CHAPTER 15

The drive back to CIS was uneventful and I spent the time mulling over what I had just learned from Carl Simmons. If Megan's parents had so thoroughly disowned her four or five years ago, it was unlikely they would have anything to do with her murder. I supposed it was possible that, if Megan forcibly tried to reenter their lives there could have been a violent reaction, but that seemed improbable. For one thing, Megan was killed at *her* place, not theirs, and I couldn't see the parents who had disowned their daughter so completely suddenly looking her up. For another, there wasn't enough time between when I dropped her off to when she died for something that serious to develop with the parents. It might be possible, but, unless it had already been brewing, I thought it was not likely.

Back in the office, I bought a Diet Coke from the machine and made my way back to my cubicle. Rob and Dex were not in evidence. Just as well, because I was not in much mood for chit-chat and I suspected that Rob at least would have been in a bantering mood. I spent the rest of the afternoon plowing through the mountain of emails that had come in over the week I'd been out. There were still dozens of unread messages in my inbox by the time I was ready to leave.

Champ was ecstatic to see me, as evidenced by the helicopter tail rotating at its maximum speed. After walking him for a good half hour, I returned to the condo, filled the dog food dish, and put out fresh water in his bowl. Then I walked slowly down the hall. I wanted to see Jenna. In truth, I *needed* to see her.

Jenna opened her door promptly to my gentle knock. I could tell she was happy to see me just by looking at her, and I felt the tight ball in my gut relax. Only then did I realize how anxious I'd been about this reunion. She gently slipped her arms around me and kissed me deeply, hungrily. After a long embrace, she stepped back and invited me in.

I chuckled to myself when I saw she already had two wineglasses on the coffee table, because I sensed, no, *knew*, that she'd been anticipating this evening as much as I had. I said nothing while she poured a chilled Riesling and set out a plate of finger sandwiches.

"You're quite the hostess," I offered.

She laughed. I was hoping you'd come by and I wanted to be ready. I didn't want to seem pushy by asking you over again, but I was secretly afraid you wouldn't."

Now it was my turn to laugh. "And *I* worried you might not want me to come."

We both continued to giggle like a couple of teenagers. This time, we sat snuggled together on the sofa. No chairs for us tonight.

We made some small talk for a while, then I steered the conversation in the direction I needed it to go. "Jenna," I began, "I have a hard time putting into words how much Friday night meant to me, but I have to admit that the big picture isn't clear to me. I don't know if you want to start a relationship or…" My voice tailed off.

Jenna smiled, then said in mock accusation, "You couldn't decide if I just shagged you for the night or what, could you?"

"I have to confess I didn't know quite *what* to make of it. I know what I *want* it to be."

"And that is?" she asked?

I decided to go for broke. "What I really want is for something more meaningful than a one-night stand or friends with benefits. I almost don't dare to hope that you want the same thing." There. It was out on the table.

She smiled again, an encouraging smile. "My ex was a louse, a shitheel," she said, "but I did miss having a *relationship*. Looking back, I don't think I ever had a true relationship with Ben. He was there, physically, but I've come to see that he wasn't there emotionally. I had a feeling that you might have a similar hole in your life."

"Spot on," I replied. "Unlike you, I was fortunate enough to be gifted with a wonderful wife and a terrific marriage. When Lisa died, it left a hole in my life, an emptiness that I never have been able to fill. Then, when you and I were together Friday, when we made love, I felt complete for the first time in four years."

Jenna buried her face on my shoulder and gently kissed my neck, sending shockwaves up and down my spine. I took my arm from around her, reached over and picked up the two wineglasses, and handed one to her. We gently clinked them together and I said, "To you,"

"No," she replied softly, "to *us*."

We sipped the Riesling for a moment. "Like I said," she continued, "Ben was never fully invested emotionally in our marriage. When I say I wanted a relationship, I didn't mean that I wanted the kind of relationship Ben and I had, I wanted the kind we *should* have had and didn't, one like it sounds like you and Lisa had."

"You deserve that," I said. "We both do."

Then I tacked. "I suppose you realize how much older I am than you are." I sure hated to toss a wet blanket over such a promising conversation, but the elephant in the room refused to be ignored.

Jenna flashed her gray-blue eyes at me and smiled her most endearing smile. "I have a general idea and, before you go any further, it doesn't matter."

"You say that now. Will you still feel that way when I'm a doddering old man?"

"I might be a doddering old woman first! We might both be gone before either of us gets to the doddering stage. Who knows? Who can say? Life has no guarantees. I believe in *preparing* for the future but I'm not a *slave* to it. We can enjoy being together while we can and let that part of the future take care of itself."

"My daughter was telling me almost the same thing exactly yesterday.

"She sounds like an amazingly wise young lady."

"She is. She wants to meet you, by the way. She was rather insistent about it."

I squeezed Jenna's hand and we both sat in comfortable silence for a bit as I basked in the pleasure of simply being with this remarkable woman.

We must have both been hungry because we attacked the plate of finger sandwiches with gusto and it was soon empty. Then Jenna surprised me by bringing out a plate of freshly baked cookies.

"Perfect!" I said, Thinking: *What did I do to deserve a woman like this?*

Jenna sat down and snuggled up to me once more. Then we fed each other cookies from the plate. We really were like two teenagers in love, and it was wonderful.

That night, we made love again and slept a deep, restful sleep until morning.

CHAPTER 16

When we woke the next morning, it was only Wednesday. That meant I was due back at the office and Jenna had her first shift of the week at the hospital. She was already out of the shower and dressed in her scrubs by the time I got up. I found her at the kitchen table eating oatmeal. She had a bowl set out for me as well.

Last night, we had other things on our mind and I never told her about my visit with Carl Simmons. Over bowls of oatmeal, I recounted my lunchtime conversation with him. Jenna frowned when I told her about how Megan's parents had cut her off completely. In the end, though, she agreed it was unlikely that the parents had anything to do with her tragic death.

Now I abruptly changed the subject. "Do you ever think about having pets?"

"Pets?" A quizzical expression played across her face.

"More specifically, a couple of cats. Megan had two cats. The brother has them now but can't keep them and he's looking to find them a new home."

She thought for a minute. "I suppose I could. You know, I used to have a cat when I was a child and I had one when I was married. She died right before Ben and I split up." She paused, then, "But pets can be a lot of responsibility."

"In my experience, as long as they're healthy, cats don't require much maintenance." Lisa had had a cat before we got married, but her parents were so fond of it that we left it with them. That was the sum total of my cat-keeping experience and it was second-hand. But something told me that Smoke and Mimosa would do well with Jenna and vice versa.

"I think I'd like to try it. They could keep me company when you're not around." She grinned at me. God, how I loved to see her smile.

I was finally starting to settle back into my routine at Comprehensive Information Systems. By midmorning I had managed to work my way through the last of the old emails and was able to concentrate on my project work. Brad had sent me a list of servers that needed new storage, so I worked on these until it was time for lunch.

Up to now, I usually skipped breakfast in the mornings and was ready and raring to go the minute the lunch hour arrived. Having shared breakfast with Jenna today, the edge of desperation wasn't there, although I was still hungry. I made my way down to the cafeteria, ordered and paid for a roast beef sandwich, and carried it back to my desk. As I ate, I sipped on the Diet Coke I got from the vending machine. The break in routine gave me a chance to think about Megan.

I wasn't sure why, but I couldn't let go of Megan's death. I knew it was a case for the police. I didn't have any experience as a detective, I had no special investigative skills, and certainly no official authority or contacts in the law enforcement community. It was insane to think that I could solve the case before the police did, yet I couldn't seem to get it out of my head and leave it alone either. Maybe it was because somebody that was close to me had been murdered. But people are murdered all the time and *their* friends and relatives don't go into Sherlock Holmes mode. I couldn't explain it. But I couldn't let it go.

I had learned from the *Dispatch* and the TV news that the crime scene had been singularly bereft of forensic evidence. No fingerprints, no hairs or fibers, nothing with DNA. Either this guy—and it almost had to be a man—was incredibly careful or else he was extremely lucky. Or the CSI team was sloppy, which I doubted was the case. Even the murder weapon, a length of two-by-two, had proven to be untraceable. It was just a piece of wood with nothing to tie it to anybody besides Megan herself. The blood spatter showed that she had been killed right there in her living room and, although there were what appeared to be footprints, the killer evidently wore some sort of covering on his shoes because there were no patterns to tie the marks to an individual shoe. Was this a killer experienced enough that he knew how to avoid leaving evidence? Or was it just dumb luck?

My goal was to learn as much about the crime as I could without bumping up against the police investigation. The last thing I needed was for the detective duo of Vickers and Tosca to come down on me for interfering with their case.

I decided that my next move would be to look up Megan's ex-boyfriend, Liam Murphy. I had no phone number for him and had no idea where he lived. He was a cable TV installer, so he worked out of a truck instead of an office. But Megan had mentioned that he liked to hang out in one of the dive bars near campus. I would start there. There are a lot of campus bars, but not so many that I couldn't cover them all in a reasonably short time.

Something else had been nagging at me: surveillance video. In post-9/11 America, surveillance cameras are ubiquitous, and the odds were more than good that Megan's apartment building had video from the period before and after the murder. Why hadn't anybody said anything about video? Did video not exist or, if it did, did it not show anything? I resolved to dig into this question after I tracked down Mr. Murphy.

I finished my sandwich and sipped the last of the Coke. I knew I wasn't done with this case. Not by a long shot.

CHAPTER 17

Manny's has long been a fixture on High Street north of the Ohio State University campus. It caters to a beer crowd, although there is an impressive array of liquor bottles behind the bar. These, I suspect, are mostly for patrons who order shots with their beers or for those who like their liquor straight. Order a cosmopolitan here and you'll probably send the barkeep scurrying for her Old Mr. Boston Bartender's Guide. There is no menu and no food. This is a place where people come to drink, period. And even though the patrons were almost exclusively Ohio State students, Megan's former boyfriend liked to hang out here. Megan herself had mentioned that on one of our commutes. If I wanted to talk to Mr. Murphy, I figured this was as good a place as any to start.

Entering the front door, I faced a row of booths along the wall to my left, four or five tables in the middle, and a bar with a dozen high, backless barstools along the right. The woman behind the bar was somewhere between tall and short, not young, not old, and neither ugly nor pretty. She was, in fact, almost perfectly nondescript. Even her clothes were unremarkable. I do remember she had reddish hair that might have even been her natural color but in the dim light, it was impossible to tell.

I spotted my quarry sitting mid-bar drinking Pabst Blue Ribbon beer straight from the can. He was wearing faded jeans, a John Deere sweatshirt, and a billed cap with some logo I didn't recognize. I quietly sat down next to him and ordered a draft Budweiser. Now, Bud at the ballpark is one thing, but I'm usually not much for beer at other times. Beer looked like my best opportunity for keeping a low profile in Manny's though. Ms. Nondescript laid a heavy, hexagonal mug on the bar in front of me and I took a sip.

I had to be careful with my next move. Liam Murphy is a redheaded giant about half a foot taller than me. He outweighs me by twenty or thirty pounds and his weight is mostly muscle; mine is not. If I pissed him off, I might not get the information I wanted and I could possibly end up getting hurt in the process.

Since we'd never actually met, I started with an introduction. "Liam, I'm Greg West. I was a friend of Megan's."

The redheaded giant turned toward me and, with some effort, focused piercing green eyes on me. *"How's that for coincidence,"* I thought. Megan had similar green eyes.

"Yeah, whaddya want?" His manner was not what you would call sociable.

"Like I said, I was a friend of Megan's. We worked at the same place and drove to work together. I'm trying to find out what I can about what happened to her."

"Ain't the cops doin' that?" It was barely past five-thirty, and he was already half in the bag.

"Well, let's just say that I'd like to try to help them. I understand you talked to the police?"

"Fuckers kept me in the poke for almost a week. Missed her funeral. Fuckers!" Obviously, my questions and these memories were stirring him up, the opposite of what I intended.

"Tell me," I continued gently, "about Megan. I know what *I* knew about her. Will you tell me what *you* knew?" I took another sip of my Budweiser. Or it might have been a gulp.

He looked down at the floor. "Wunnerful girl. I really fucked that one up! She pissed me off and I popped her one. Knew I shouldna, but I did anyway. She kicked me out. Guess I deserved it." He snapped his head up and looked me in the eye. "But I didn't kill her. Tole the cops that, but they didn't believe me. They knew I hit her and kept harpin' on that." It was not hard to imagine that Tosca would have handled that interview with his usual finesse.

By now, Murphy's can and my mug were empty. I ordered two more beers, perhaps not the best prescription for the redheaded giant, but I thought a little extra lubrication might help my cause. The nondescript barkeep brought the beers and I continued pumping Murphy.

"Did the cops ask you where you were Friday?" I thought phrasing the question that way might get him talking about the police interview rather than considering *me* the interviewer.

Murphy picked up the cocktail napkin sitting on the bar in front of him and started toying with it. "Course they did," he replied. I got a brother lives down close to Pataskala, so when Megan tole me to get out, I went and crashed at his place. He ain't working just now, so he and I, we spent the weekend drinkin' and watchin' football on the TV." A belch escaped and he took another guzzle from the can of Blue Ribbon. "Guess it ain't much of a whatcha call an alibi, least not accordin' to the cops, but that's where I was and what we did."

"No one else see you?"

"Nah, ya see, Sean's ol' lady, she left him 'bout six months ago, so we had the place to ourselves." I did not find the brother's matrimonial problems to be a big surprise. Megan was a smart girl. How she ended up with this bumpkin was a mystery to me. On the other hand, while he might be an ignorant hayseed, that didn't make him a murderer, and I just wasn't getting a murderer vibe from Liam Murphy.

"Look, mister, uh what was ya name again?"

"West. Greg West."

"Look, Mr. West, I know I fucked up with Megan. My daddy always tole me that when you hit a woman you stopped bein' a man." To say hearing that bit of philosophy from the redheaded giant surprised me was a colossal understatement. He continued, "But ya see, I'd got inta trouble at work and had a few brewskis on the way home. Megan got in my shit about it an' I got mad an' punched her. Just once, but I knew right then I shouldn't'a. Too late, though. She tole me to get my shit and get out."

"And you did get out?"

"Yeah, I tossed some clothes in a duffle an' booked to my brother's. He always tole me I could crash with him anytime I needed to."

"And then the police picked you up?"

Murphy was now shredding the cocktail napkin, tearing it into small pieces. "Yeah, cops grabbed me sometime Sunday afternoon, late. Took me down to that big cop house downtown an' gave me the turd degree." I doubted he had any concept of what the third degree really was, but I let it pass. "Kept at it all Sunday night an' most of Monday."

"Wait," I interjected, "they questioned you after you'd been drinking?"

"Sure. Didn't make no difference to me. And I didn't want no lawyer, neither. I didn't do nuthin, so I weren't worried."

I thought about the number of innocent people who blunder into prison by failing to appreciate the pitfalls of navigating a police interrogation unassisted by legal counsel.

My mug was still half full, but Murphy's can was obviously empty. I ordered him a refill and pressed on. "Did they arrest you or just question you?"

"They ran the full boat. Mugshot, prints, everything."

"But then they let you go?" Of course, they did, or we wouldn't be talking, but I wanted to get his perspective.

"Yeah, tole me they weren't gonna keep me on accounta not finding any whatcha call physical evidence. No prints or nuthin. It was that lady cop that made 'em turn me loose. That skinny Eye-talian cop woulda kept me till hell froze." I stifled a chuckle. I could almost see Vickers and Tosca.

"And you didn't go back to Megan's? Did you, like, forget something and go back to get it?"

"Nah, Sean and I was partyin' an' I didn't pay no 'tention to what I did or didn't bring with me." That had the ring of truth. "Ya know," he continued, "I know *I* didn't kill her, and if she hadn't'a thrown me out, I might'a been able to, you know, prevent this." I swear tears welled up in the big lug's eyes. And he was probably right. Assuming he didn't kill her, and I was becoming more and more convinced that he hadn't, he might well have saved Megan's life if he had still been with her. Or maybe he would have ended up as the second victim. Who knew?

The cocktail napkin was now a pile of paper lint. I paid for the beers, including the ones he'd had before I showed up, adding a generous tip for Ms. Nondescript. I thanked him for his time. "Liam," I said, "I know this has been difficult for you, but I really want to thank you for talking to me. I'm not sure how just yet, but I believe what you've told me will help me, and maybe you, too."

"Ah, no problem, Mr., what was ya name again?"

"West. Greg West." The guy apparently had the memory of a goldfish.

"No problem, Mr. West. You can find me here most anytime."

I didn't doubt that I could. With that, I hoisted myself off the barstool and walked out of Manny's onto the High Street sidewalk.

CHAPTER 18

Rob was in an elevated state of excitement when I arrived at the office the next morning. I barely had time to sit down in my chair before he poked his head inside my cube. "Yo! Greg. You just missed the guys from Loss Prevention."

"Yeah, so what?" I thought of Loss Prevention as a bunch of bean counters whose main purpose was to make life as difficult as possible for those of us with actual work to do.

"Well," Rob half-whispered in his most conspiratorial tone, "Story is that Megan had signed out a laptop to work on it. She does that desktop thing, you know." I knew. I also noticed that Rob used the present tense when talking about Megan. I wasn't the only one having difficulty with her death. "Anyway," he continued, "they went to get it and couldn't find it at her desk or anywhere in her cube."

I tried to brush Rob off, but by now, Dex and Henry had showed up. Staring at my screens with my best look of concentration, I mumbled "I'm sure it'll turn up. It's probably in her apartment."

"That's what the L.P. guys thought, too, but the cops said they didn't find a laptop there."

Intrigued, now, I looked up and asked, "Do you know if they found Megan's own laptop?"

"I don't think so. Everybody's in a tizzy"

"Two laptops aren't even a blip on the radar for this company. We have thousands of laptops"

Rob moved closer and dropped his voice further. "Sure, we do, but the L.P. guys are scared shitless that some bad guy somewhere will steal information off 'em. They've even got old Battenslag in a lather over it."

"What's the big deal? All our laptops have boot-drive encryption.

"*Most* of them do but not all, at least that's what a buddy I have in InfoSec tells me." Rob seemed to know somebody everywhere.

Henry nodded in agreement. "Yeah, that's true. There was a foul-up when we introduced encryption and a bunch of laptops got missed."

"How many is a 'bunch'?" I asked?

"Oh, maybe twenty or thirty or so."

I mulled over his news about the unencrypted drives. Information Security had the responsibility of protecting company data from theft or unauthorized disclosure. According to policy, *all* company laptops should have their boot drives encrypted. Twenty or thirty laptops was a few, not a bunch, but still, if an unencrypted laptop led to a data breach, it could easily be a resume-generating event for someone in InfoSec.

"I can see why InfoSec would have their boxers in a bunch," I said. Then a new thought hit me. "You know, I think the cops believe that whoever killed Megan didn't take anything from her apartment. What if they *did* take a laptop or two?"

"That could be a big, fat, hairy bad deal," Dex offered, while Henry nodded in agreement, "especially if one or both were unencrypted."

I asked, "Any idea whose laptop is missing"

Rob piped up, "No. Desktop Support had a bunch that they were going to work on, but I don't think anybody's figured out who the missing one—or ones—belong to." Rob was a fount of company gossip and his sources were usually impeccable.

Suddenly, over Rob's shoulder, the dyspeptic face of Detective Tosca appeared. "West, we're looking for a couple of laptops."

I groaned inwardly, as the trio of Rob, Dex, and Henry scattered, scurrying away as unobtrusively as they could. "I know nothing of laptops, detective. As you can see, mine is right here."

"All right, wiseass. I just wanted to know if you knew anything about their whereabouts."

"No, I do not. I'm guessing you think there is some tie-in to the murder?"

"Let me ask the questions," Tosca grumped. "You know anything about 'em or not? Where's Miss Simmons's laptop?"

"The last time I saw Megan," I replied slowly, "she was carrying a backpack. It may or may not have had a laptop in it. She didn't open it and I didn't look inside it."

Tosca didn't like that answer, but I guess he decided he wasn't going to get a better one. "You find that laptop, you call us, you hear?"

"Of course, detective. I promise I will." I tried to sound sincere and not too sarcastic.

While kibbitzing with Rob, Dex, and Henry and dealing with Tosca, the unread messages in my inbox had swollen back to epic proportions and I spent the rest of the morning plowing through them. A few were genuinely important: requests from users, alerts from arrays and servers that needed something fixed, and an announcement concerning the paid holiday schedule for the upcoming season. Much of it, though, was simply chaff. But I had to wade through the chaff anyway to extract the few kernels of wheat.

If wading through email sounds dull, the afternoon was even duller. I spent most of it investigating failed backups. Every company of any size backs up the data on their computers. That is, they copy the data to another location, indexing it so that it is easily retrievable. That way, if Susie in accounting accidentally waxes the spreadsheet she's been working on for a week, I can retrieve a copy that is recent enough so that she doesn't have to start from scratch.

It sounds simple in theory, but backup systems are incredibly complex and not a day goes by that at least a few servers fail to back up completely or correctly. Sometimes they don't back up at all. The reasons vary. Most of the failures have simple causes. But fixing them isn't always simple. Investigating and resolving these problems can be time-consuming—and boring.

My eyes were starting to glaze over by the time I called it a day and left the office. I fired up the Mustang and guided it out of the parking lot. Jenna was studying for some sort of certification exam she had to take for work, so I had not seen her last night. I was aching to see her now. I sped along I-670 until I reached the usual knot at the Third and Fourth Street exits, then crept through downtown until I reached my garage.

Jenna would still be studying—the exam was tomorrow—so I wouldn't stay long, but I wanted to see her even if it was only for a short visit. I stopped at her door and tapped gently. There was a pause just long enough for her to look through the peephole and identify her visitor, then the door opened. She was wearing a long, snug T-shirt and, I suspected, nothing else. I tried not to stare at her breasts pressing against the taut fabric, but she saw me and laughed. "You're peeking!"

"Busted," I said.

"Come in, you! I just have a minute, you know"

"Yes, I know, and I won't stay long. But I just *had* to see you tonight." We caught each other up on our days and I filled her in on my conversation with Liam Murphy last night and the laptop puzzle of this morning.

"So, there are *two* laptops missing?" she asked.

"Looks like it, although I don't know that either one is for sure."

"Wonder if that's important?"

"Yeah, me too. It might mean nothing, or it might mean everything."

We said our goodbyes and I left her sitting cross-legged on the floor poring over her study materials, which she had arrayed around her on the furniture and the floor. I took in one last look, savoring the gray-blue eyes twinkling at me and the honey blonde hair pulled back into a loose ponytail. Then I left and closed the door behind me, first making sure that I locked it.

That simple act born of long habit made me think of something. Nobody had *broken into* Megan's apartment, at least not through the front door. I was there. I saw the door. It was intact, just unlatched. The *Dispatch* and the TV stations hadn't said anything about forced entry, and neither had the police. Did that mean Megan knew her killer or did he get in with a ruse, posing as a deliveryman, perhaps?

Megan was a rather trusting soul who always tried to see the best in people. I suspected that was at least part of why she made such singularly bad choices in boyfriends. On the other hand, she wasn't naïve. She'd lived in the center of a mid-sized city and knew the score. She was meticulous about locking her door when she was home. We'd had a drive-time conversation about that very subject, and I'd seen for myself that she was diligent about locking the door on the one or two occasions I was in her apartment. She kept her front door locked.

One thought led to another. The TV stations and the *Dispatch* all said there had been no sexual assault, either. When I first discovered her body, though, I'd assumed from its nude state and the posing, that the killer had a sexual motivation. If that was the case, either he stopped short of rape or the paper and TV stations had kept a lid on it. It is common practice for the police to hold back some details of a crime. It helps them weed out the "confessing Sams" that often come out of the woodwork after a major or highly publicized crime. But to my knowledge, those details held back are usually minor and subtle, a category that didn't fit sexual assault.

I pondered these mysteries within the mystery. How did the killer get in? Why was she posed suggestively and naked? Most of all, *who the hell killed Megan?*

Champ was waiting for me at the door and was eager to take his evening constitutional. Today his tail was swinging from side to side, like a batter warming up in the on-deck circle. It was still a manifest display of satisfaction and joy. Ah, how pleasant it must be to be a dog.

CHAPTER 19

I wanted to find out if Megan's attacker broke in or if she let him in. I reread the newspaper articles I'd saved, and the ones that mentioned it did say that there was no sign of forced entry. I was sure I remembered all the TV channels saying the same thing. The press sometimes gets it wrong, though, so I really wanted to find out from the horse's mouth, so to speak. I knew that meant a call to either Tosca or Vickers and I also knew that they would easily recognize my voice and the game would be up.

I expounded on my quandary to Rob and Dexter the next morning. "I'd really like to have the cops either confirm that there was no forced entry or tell me I'm full of shit," I said, "but I can't see them telling me anything."

"You still trying to be the master detective?" Rob thought I should drop it and leave matters to the police.

"I can't let it go, Rob. It's got hold of me somehow. And another thing. The way I found her, I thought she must've been raped. The news people are saying there was no sexual assault, though. I'd like to settle *that* question, too."

"Could you call one of the cops and pretend to be a reporter or something?"

"Not a bad idea, Rob, but they know my voice. Maybe you could make the call for me?"

"No *way*, man! I'd choke." Rob was just nervous enough that he probably would.

Dexter spoke up. "I'll do it. It's no big deal."

"Great, Dex! Thank you!" I was beginning to think this might actually work.

By now, Henry had joined the three of us hovering around Dex's cube.

Dexter sat down at his desk, harrumphed a couple of times, gravely donned his phone headset, and dialed police headquarters. Summoning a *basso profundo* I didn't know he possessed, he spoke into the instrument, "Detective Vickers, please." He was taking the easier route choosing Vickers over Tosca; I would have, too.

"Detective Vickers, this is Franklin Snow with Channel 3 in Cleveland. We've been covering the story of that girl that was murdered down there in Columbus last week, and I had a question or two."

Rob and I heard faint squawking coming from the headphones. "No, Cleveland. Channel 3. WKYC, Cleveland's News Leader." Nice touch. If Detective Vickers knew anything about C-town, using the call letters of a real TV station lent an air of credibility.

More squawking, then, "Detective Vickers, there's one thing I really need to nail down before I can file my story, and I want to make sure I get it right. One of our sources tells us that the killer broke a back window to get in the girl's apartment. Can you confirm that?"

Breaking in through a window would have been quite a trick. Megan's apartment was on the sixth floor; it would take a hook and ladder to reach her back window from the street.

The squawking was more vigorous and more prolonged.

"You don't say. So, there was absolutely *no* evidence of forced entry? I see. And from that, do you conclude that she knew her killer? Yes, ma'am, I understand. No, thank you for your cooperation.

"Oh, one more thing," he added. "I understand from the way the body was positioned that the killer might have had a sexual motive. Can you comment on that?"

Again, more squawking.

"Yes ma'am. that fits with our information, too. Thank you for your time, detective."

As soon as Dex hung up, Rob and I could no longer contain ourselves and we burst out laughing. Henry soon joined our merriment and, finally, so did Dexter himself. "If CIS ever finds out what a lazy slob you are and fires you," I joked, "you've got a second career waiting. So, what's the scoop?"

"The scoop, as you say," he answered, "is that the police found no evidence of forced entry. Ms. Vickers would not comment on whether that meant the victim knew the killer, but there was no sexual assault and no forced entry. She was quite positive on both points."

"That raises almost as many questions as it answers," I mused. "Other than the ex-boyfriend, I can't see anybody Megs knew as wanting to kill her. And I'm really starting to doubt that the boyfriend did, either."

"Hey, guys," Rob interjected. "Friend of mine, he's a cameraman for Channel 6 news. He was part of the team that covered the murder. He told me one of the reporters got hold of the security camera video from the apartment building. Think you could learn anything from that?" Despite himself, Rob was getting sucked into this case, too.

I was barely able to suppress my excitement at this news. "You know, that could be extremely helpful. Who's your friend?" Rob scribbled a name and phone number on a Post-it and handed it to me. Folding it in half so that the sticky side touched the back of the note, I tucked it in my pants pocket. "Thanks, dude," I murmured.

"No sweat. I'll give him a heads-up that you'll be calling him."

"That would be great, too."

Rob looked up and nodded toward the approaching figure of Brad Carter. "Time to get back to work, Sherlock," he whispered with a grin. By the time Brad reached our work area, Henry had left and Brad, Dex, and I had our noses pointed to our screens, the very picture of concentration.

"You're not fooling me, you goof-offs. I saw your coffee klatch break up at the last second before I got here." The twinkle in Brad's eyes showed amusement rather than anger. Brad was the best kind of boss, one that trusted you to do your job and left you pretty much alone so long as you finished what you were supposed to do.

"Sorry, Brad," I said, "I guess it's my fault."

Brad pulled a chair from a vacant cube into my cube and sat down. He spoke to me in a low voice so that neither Rob nor Dexter could hear. "Greg, I know you've had a helluva shock. Are you sure you're all right? Do you need some more time off?"

"Is there a problem, Brad?"

Brad's left hand began stroking his shiny head. "No, not at all, but I *am* concerned about you. You know, finding the girl, the police questioning, the funeral. Getting over these things takes time."

"It *was* a shock," I replied, "and I can't say I'm over it, but I'm probably as over it as I'm going to be for a while. Besides, I have someone helping me."

"Did you see a therapist, a counselor?"

"No," I said, thinking of Jenna, "a friend, but it helps nonetheless."

"Good. I just wanted you to know that if you need more time, you can take it."

"Thanks, Brad. I appreciate that, I really do. But I think the best thing for me now is to try to get back into as normal a routine as I can." Driving to work in the morning and home in the evening without Megan was far from routine, and it would take a long time to get over *that*.

Brad replaced the chair in the empty cube and went back to his office.

I tried to concentrate on work the rest of the day, I really did, but Megan kept getting in the way. The lack of forced entry really bothered me. Try as I might, I couldn't come up with anyone who would have wanted to kill her, much less someone she would have let in. The more I thought about him, the more I discounted Liam Murphy. Whatever else he was, he did not impress me as a serial abuser. When I talked to him, he was neither angry nor vengeful. He had let his temper get the best of him once and seemed to be genuinely sorry. Of course, there was always the possibility that he was putting on an act for me, but I doubted the redheaded giant was academy award material.

At the same time, Megan absolutely did the right thing breaking off with him then and there. So many battered women keep going back to their abusers and it was to her credit that she made a clean break after the first blow. The ironic thing is that taking an action that would normally keep her safe—ending a relationship with a man who hit her—may have indirectly caused her death. I couldn't see anybody doing much to Megan if Liam Murphy had been there. It was all terribly tragic and thinking about it left me depressed.

I turned back to my keyboard and discovered that I had daydreamed long enough for my screens to lock. I keyed in my password to unlock them and went back to work.

When lunchtime rolled around, I grabbed a pasta salad from the cafeteria and a Diet Coke from the machine and took them back to my desk to eat. I slipped Rob's Post-it out of my pocket and smoothed it out on the desk. It contained a name, Tyrone Jackson, and a phone number. When I dialed the number, I got voice mail, the kind that just reads back the number with no personal message. The voice mail message droned on for a bit, then I heard the beep.

"Mr. Jackson," I began, "My name is Greg West. I work with Rob Ford at Comprehensive Information Systems. He gave me your name and said you might be willing to talk to me about a story you recently covered. I would really appreciate it if you'd sit down with me for half an hour or so." I gave an outline of what I wanted to discuss, left my personal cell number, and hung up. Maybe he'd call, maybe he wouldn't. I had to wait to find out.

Anticipating Jackson's callback wrecked my concentration. I still had a pile of backup failures to investigate, so I decided to work on those. It was tedious and time-consuming work, but it didn't require much brainpower, which made it the perfect task for my distracted state of mind. At intervals the soft "whang" sound announced more incoming email. Routine messages I deleted or filed; the ones that required action or actual thinking I saved for later.

A couple of calls to my cell phone in midafternoon briefly raised my hopes, but they turned out to be phone spam. The first was a robocall. When the second proved to be from a live person promising to fix my credit, I barked an obscenity at him and hung up.

Even with my mind virtually in neutral, I managed to work my way through the backlog of backup failures. It may be drudge work, it's necessary drudge work. I felt a bit of satisfaction at using my less-than-alert state to get it done. The whangs of the email alert tone had tailed off, an indication that the end of the workday was near. Seeing that it was nearly four o'clock, I had just about decided to bag it and go home when my cell phone rang again.

"Hello."

"Mr. West? This is Ty Jackson returning your call." At last!

"Thanks for calling me back, Mr. Jackson. I was hoping you'd be willing to meet with me to discuss a story that I understand you helped cover."

"That's what your message said. You wanted to talk about the Megan Simmons murder, right?"

"Yes." I could almost hear him frowning over the telephone.

"You know, Mr. West," he began, "when you do what I do, you see a lot of bad and messy crime scenes. This one was one of the messiest. Sure, I'd be glad to talk to you."

Inwardly, I breathed a huge sigh of relieve. "Can you meet now, in about half an hour?"

Jackson agreed to meet me at Dempsey's in thirty minutes. I described myself and told him I'd be wearing a black jacket with the logo of one of our computer equipment vendors on it. Thanking him, I hung up and bolted for the exit.

CHAPTER 20

Dempsey's is a Columbus fixture located on South High Street at the corner of Mound. Its strategic location a block from the Franklin County Municipal Court and across the street from the Common Pleas Court make it a lunchtime and after-hours favorite of the courthouse crowd. The place was just starting to fill up with lawyerly looking people when I entered. A stocky African American man sitting at the bar waved me onto an empty tall bar chair next to him. I sat down on the proffered chair. He stuck out a hand the size of a bear paw and introduced himself as Ty Jackson.

It was impossible to determine Jackson's age. His round head was completely devoid of hair, primarily, I observed, from natural baldness. What would have been a fringe of hair around the edges, he'd shaved off. His face was intelligent-looking and gave an aura of a man who looked at life a little quizzically and with an easy sense of humor. Although he had the build of a manual laborer, he was dressed for an office. A glass of what I assumed was bourbon or scotch with a single large ice cube sat on the bar in front of him.

I opened the conversation. "I can't thank you enough for agreeing to see me, Mr. Jackson, especially on such short notice."

"Please, call me Ty," he said.

"And call me Greg," I replied. "Let me tell you why I wanted to talk to you. Megan Simmons was my friend. We worked at the same company and carpooled together for a couple of years. And I was the one who discovered her."

Jackson looked thoughtful.

"Anyway," I continued, "I know I should probably keep my nose out of it, but I just can't let this go. There's a cop poking around the case, a Detective Tosca, but I don't think he's getting anywhere."

Jackson laughed at the mention of Tosca's name. "I know Tosca. He's been riding with Sharona Vickers for a couple of years, now. *She's* the real brains of that outfit."

"I gathered as much."

"He's really a pretty decent guy when you get to know him and a respectable detective, but he's under a lot of pressure and his technique lacks finesse. Once he gets on a scent, he hangs on like a bulldog."

"Does he ever *find* the scent," I asked.

Jackson laughed a big hearty laugh. "Sure, he does. Most of the time, anyway."

I wanted to steer the conversation toward my objective. "I understand that you and one of the reporters got a good look at the crime scene. I also heard that you had access to the security camera video."

"Right on both. I've been in the TV news business for near twenty years, now, and this was one of the most gruesome murders I've ever covered. There was blood *everywhere*. Matt, the reporter, and I both nearly lost our lunch. Matt, he's covered homicides since forever and he turned green as Kermit the Frog."

"I saw the blood in the living room when I found her," I said quietly. "Was there blood anywhere else? I only saw the living room."

"Oh, yes," he replied slowly. "The bathroom was a bloody mess. I heard to cops say that the guy must have tried to clean himself up there. That sounds about right because he didn't try to clean up the living room."

That got my attention. I didn't recall reading or hearing anything about blood in the bathroom. "Yes, it *does* make sense. The killer must have been drenched in blood. Going out in public like that would be sure to get attention."

"Matt and me, we thought for sure this was a sex crime, what with her being naked and her legs spread out like that and all. But Matt, he heard from the cops that it wasn't so. At least they didn't recover any whatcha call 'biological material' from her."

"That squares with what I've heard," I agreed. "Did the place look ransacked? All I saw was the living room, but it didn't look like it had been disturbed much."

"Neat as a pin, except for all the blood and the dead girl, of course. Cops said there wasn't a fight. He must've immobilized her the first time he whacked her because they didn't find anything under her fingernails to test for DNA. And the rest of the place 'sides the bathroom and a few books and magazines on the floor was in apple-pie order."

"My friend Rob said you guys might have seen the surveillance video?" It was a question rather than a statement.

"Rob told me you were interested in that. Sure, we did," he said, "but it wasn't much help. Matt, he got a copy from the cops and we watched it together."

"What could you see from it? Surely it must have told the police *something*."

"See for yourself," he said. He reached a bear paw into a shirt pocket and fished out a flash drive, which he handed to me. "I figured you'd want to see it, you bein' interested in the case and all. Keep the computer doohickey; We got dozens of 'em back at the station."

"This is fantastic! Thank you!" I wanted to jump up and dance across the floor, but I restrained myself.

"Matt didn't see anything he thought was useful and I guess neither did the cops. I know they liked the boyfriend for it and even hauled him in, but they couldn't make it stick. They didn't collect any physical evidence and they couldn't make an ID from the video. You'll see what I mean when you watch it. That building's only got three cameras: one on the front entrance, one on the back, and one in the lobby. Nothing inside in the elevators or on the floors. Couldn't see the guy go in the girl's place, but he had to be the one."

"I want to see the video myself, of course, but was *anyone* close to the case on it?"

Jackson scratched his chin. "Not really. All you could tell was it was a big guy, but he'd dressed so's you couldn't see any details. Everybody else looked like they lived there. Cops were going to try to identify everybody in the videos, but they were really disappointed. Guess they were hoping they could ID the perp from the security video. Matt, he said cops pulled video from buildings in the neighborhood but came up with squat."

"Do you know if the neighbors heard anything?"

"Not that I know. If they did, the cops didn't say so, at least while we were there. You know how it is, nobody sees anything, and nobody hears anything. You know what I think, I think the guy conked her as soon as he got in the place and didn't make much noise for anyone to hear.

'Course it's pretty obvious he hit her more than once. The poor girl was a mess."

I remembered the scene in that apartment and my stomach flipped a couple of times. "Yes, I saw that. Did you see anything else, anything at all?"

"Can't think of anything I haven't already told you."

"How about a laptop? Did you see any laptops?"

"No nothing like that. She had a TV, nice one, too, but no other electronics that I saw. I think the cops found a cell phone charging in her bedroom, but that was it."

The only significant piece of information I gained from this interview was the flash drive with the security videos. I doubted I could spot anything in them that trained police detectives couldn't see, but I was determined to try. I thanked Jackson and walked out onto High Street with the precious flash drive stowed securely in my pocket.

CHAPTER 21

I now had something to investigate. The flash drive with the security camera video could either prove to be significant or be a dead end, although I feared it would be the latter.

It was nearly time for Jenna's shift at the hospital to be over. She was bound to be tired and we hadn't made plans for the evening. I texted her that I had some things to work on tonight, that she was welcome to join me if she wanted to, but that I'd understand if she didn't. A few minutes later, she texted back and said that she was exhausted and would probably go to bed soon after she got home. At the end of the message was a little kissy face emoji. I'd have plenty of time to work, although I would miss seeing her.

Champ and I took a short walk before returning to the condo. It was raw and damp today and not pleasant weather to be outside. Champ didn't seem to mind me truncating his evening stroll.

The video was easy. There were three sizable files on the flash drive, all with a file extension of "MP4." MP4 is one of the more common video formats and I had no trouble selecting a program that would play them. I started with the file name *lobby.mp4*. As I expected, the view was of the lobby of Megan's apartment building looking toward the entrance doors. From the view angle, I judged that the camera was situated just above the elevator bank. The picture quality was decent but not great. Colors appeared more faded than vivid and the focus seemed to me to be a little fuzzy. Nor was the motion completely smooth. Rather, watching gave the impression of flipping through a stack of still photos instead of free-flowing motion.

I sped the player up to three times normal playback speed. I wanted to get to the relevant part without zooming past it. I could slow the playback when I reached the part I wanted. People came and went through the lobby entrance in rapid, herky-jerky fashion. Then I saw him. The figure opening the door at 7:51:14 p.m. *had* to be man I was looking for. I immediately understood the difficulty of making an identification from that video.

The man appeared to be tall, although it was hard to tell for sure. Unlike your run-of-the-mill 7-Eleven, the lobby didn't have height markers stenciled on the door jambs, but it looked like he was taller than most of the other people I'd seen go through those doors. Besides being tall, he was bulky, built like a defensive tackle. At least I *assumed* he was built like a defensive tackle. It was impossible to see his true build because of the long loose coat he wore that came nearly to his ankles. He might have just been fat. A hoodie he wore under the coat covered most of his head and a large western-style hat obscured his face. It had been chilly the evening of Megan's murder, but this guy was dressed for the North Pole and his appearance screamed, "Disguise!" There was something unnatural about his movement, too, which seemed closer to rolling that walking. In that getup and with that gait, he looked like a floating tent.

I moved the position marker back to the point where the Mystery Man opened the door and paused it there. Then I examined the video carefully, frame by frame. At no point could you see any facial detail. Just to be sure, I went back and repeated the process and then did it once again for good measure. There was absolutely no view of the Mystery Man's face. I could see why the cops were disappointed. I was, too. I ran through the rest of the video at warp speed without finding anything else that looked significant.

Now that I knew the timeline, or at least the starting point, it was easy to cue up the next video to that position. This file named *back.mp4* was a view of the back door and street behind Megan's building. I watched two hours' worth of video from the 7:30 mark until 9:30, speeded up, of course. A few people came and went but nobody who remotely resembled the Mystery Man. Thinking the timestamps on the two cameras might be out of sync, I watched the entire video, twenty-four hours' worth, without seeing anything of possible interest.

The last video file, *front.mp4,* was from a camera mounted outside the building and aimed at the front door. It showed a decent view of the immediate doorway and, peripherally, a bit of the sidewalk to the left and to the right. At 7:50, the Mystery Man approached from the right. The front door and lobby cameras, at least, were time-synchronized. Single stepping through this video didn't reveal any more than the lobby video had.

I assumed that the police had identified the other people coming and going from the building or had at least tried to. As much as I wanted to do that myself, I didn't have the massive number of hours it would take nor the authority to get building residents to cooperate with me. This was one time I had to trust that Vickers and Tosca were doing their homework.

A thought then struck me with the force of a lightning bolt. I'd seen the Mystery Man go *into* the apartment building, but I hadn't seen him come *out*. Now I viewed all three video files again, from about the 7:30 mark to the end of the videos at midnight. I was right. He *hadn't* come out of the building. I wondered how Vickers and Tosca explained *that*.

CHAPTER 22

Back in the office on Monday, I had a difficult time concentrating on work. I kept mulling over the surveillance videos throughout the weekend. I even discussed it over Sunday brunch with Jenna. I couldn't get the Mystery Man out of my head and I couldn't stop trying to figure out how he got out of Megan's apartment building.

By lunchtime, I was mentally exhausted and had accomplished little in the way of actual work. I was glad to take a little break to walk over to the cafeteria, where I bought a ham sandwich, a bag of barbecue potato chips, and a bottle of Diet Coke.

The cafeteria has two parts. One side is where you select and pay for your food, while the other is the dining area. The latter is a large room with numerous tables and chairs positioned around. Some of the tables are square and others are rectangular, but all have a hard, white Formica-like material for their eating surface. Two large-screen television screens are mounted at each end of the room. One screen plays a continuous loop of company information while news or insipid daytime programs babble away on the other. Large windows line the long wall opposite the food service area with rectangular high-top tables next to them.

I was about to take my sandwich and chips back to my desk when I spotted Rob, Dex, and Henry. They were at one of the tables in the center of the room away from the televisions, eating and talking. Rob, as he frequently did, wore jeans and an Ohio State sweatshirt. Henry had on a T-shirt for some band I didn't know while Dexter wore a sweatshirt with a Nike "swoosh" logo and green cargo pants.

I almost felt overdressed in my business casual shirt and pants.

I decided to join them.

Rob spoke as I sat down. "Hey, Greg, I was just telling the guys that some of us are going to Pins after work. You want to come?"

Pins is a sort of arcade-bar that features arcade games and duck pin bowling, along with an extensive bar. Another time, I might have been tempted, but I really wasn't in the mood and I suspected Rob had the location in Dublin in mind rather than the one downtown close to me.

"Which one," I asked.

"Bridge Park." I was correct, Rob was thinking Dublin. "Dex is going."

"You both live up that way. I live downtown. How about coming to the one on Fourth Street?"

"Too hard to park downtown."

"That's not true. You can find plenty of parking in the evenings. There are two garages close by and the meters open up after the offices start to empty out"

"Okay, so there's parking, but not *free* parking."

"*Now* the truth comes out, you cheapskate," I said with a grin. "Anyway, I'll pass. I'm tired and, frankly, I'm not really in the mood for arcade games today." I looked at Henry. "You're not going?"

"No," he said, "tonight is the night I volunteer at the food pantry." Henry did volunteer work at a local food pantry *and* at a homeless shelter. Both kept him pretty much occupied, I guessed.

Dexter finally spoke up. "I bet you're just begging off so you can do more gumshoe work tonight."

I took a bite of my sandwich before answering. "No, I spent the weekend doing that and my brain is pretty much fried right now." I told them about the security camera videos and the Mystery Man.

"So, you couldn't tell anything about the guy?" Henry asked.

"No, I couldn't. He looked like a big guy, but that coat hid so much it's hard to say *what* his build really was. I assumed it was a man. The hat and hoodie hid his face completely. It *could* have even been a woman. Or Sasquatch, for all I know."

I took another bite of the sandwich and munched a couple of potato chips.

"Then I guess," Henry said, "the security cameras didn't tell the cops anything."

"That's what I gathered. They sure didn't tell *me* anything."

"So, now what?"

"I understand the police pulled video from cameras on neighboring buildings. I don't know if they got anything from those or not. They're not confiding in me."

Henry looked thoughtful.

Dexter looked squarely at me. "You just can't let go of this, can you?"

"No, Dex, I'm afraid I can't. But I think I just hit a dead end and I'm not sure where to go next."

"Well," Henry said, "*I* think you should let the cops handle it."

"I'm sure Vickers and especially Tosca would agree with you, Henry." I washed down another bite of sandwich with a swig of Diet Coke.

"You ask me," Rob said, "you're getting too tangled up in this mess. Pretty soon the cops are going to make you suspect *numero uno*."

"Detective Tosca already tried that. He couldn't run that ball very far. And I *didn't* ask you."

Rob tried to put on a pained expression but overdid it. "You're not careful," he said, "and they'll squash you."

"You're probably right, Rob, and I need *that* like a moose needs a hat rack."

CHAPTER 23

On the drive to work Tuesday, it suddenly occurred to me that I might learn something by talking with Megan's coworkers. I should have thought of that earlier, but for some reason it didn't click until now. I decided to take some time today to correct that omission. I busied myself at my desk for a bit until mid-morning when I could be reasonably certain that everyone would be in the office. Then walked upstairs to the area that was home to Desktop Support.

Desktop Support consists of half a dozen people divided into two teams. Each team has a work area consisting of a small desk for each technician and a large, well-lighted bench for working on equipment. I was pleased to see that Callie Reynolds and Saligram Rama, the two technicians that worked on Megan's team were both in, Saligram sat at his desk while Callie performed surgery on a computer at the workbench. Both were much younger than me and since our paths rarely crossed, I only knew them slightly.

Saligram was of Indian heritage. He was medium height and slender, with straight black hair and a modest mustache. He wore gold wire-rimmed glasses. He had spent almost his entire life in the States, so his English was impeccable, only the slightest trace of an accent slipping out every so often. Callie was a petite blonde who wore too much makeup but didn't need to. Her hair was short and stayed neatly in place.

I greeted them. "Callie, Saligram, how's it going?"

They looked up and Callie responded, "Same old, same old, Greg. How 'bout you?"

"Nothing new work-wise."

"I heard *that!*" Saligram responded. "Of course, we're scrambling here without Megan. Extra work for Callie and me, you know, and nobody's in a hurry to hire a replacement." There was a very slight lilt to his voice, otherwise he could have been Joe Newscaster.

"Corporate America, dude, everybody does more for less."

"Humph!" was the only response I got.

"Anyway, guys," I continued, "it's Megan I wanted to talk to you about."

Callie looked up from the workbench. "Yeah," she said, "we heard you were the one that found her. Creepy, huh?"

"Yes." I shuddered involuntarily. "But I came up here to try to find out something about the missing laptops. I'm sure you've heard about the missing laptops."

"*Heard* about them? Sure, we heard, and how! L.P. was all over our asses trying to find them. All I know is *we* don't have 'em." Saligram's manner was angry or resentful or possibly both.

"Damn straight," Callie added.

"I didn't think you did," I hastily assured them. "I assume Megan was working on one and the other was the company laptop assigned to her personally."

Saligram peered at me through his gold-rimmed glasses. "That's what Callie and I figure, too."

"So, Megan's laptop is missing and one laptop, *not* Megan's, is also missing. How would she come to be working on the missing one?"

"See that rack over there?" Saligram gestured toward something that looked like a wooden bookcase except that instead of shelves, it had angled slots. Some slots held laptop computers while others were empty. "Somebody brings a laptop in for service, we log it in and assign it a bin number over there. The bin number goes in the service ticket. When one of us pulls a ticket out of the queue, it tells us which bin number has the laptop we need to work on. Unless it's a house call."

"House calls" were tickets for problems that the technicians could easily fix at the caller's desk. That was how I first met Megan. She came to my desk to replace a flaky memory module.

"The last day Megan was here, did you have any house calls?" I asked.

"None that I remember," Saligram said. "How about you, Callie? You remember any house calls that day?"

"No."

I was getting information. None of it was helping but I persevered. "Do you remember if anybody brought laptops in that day?"

Callie thought for a minute. "I don't think so. We were working through the backlog."

"Do you log in all the laptops yourself?"

"Some of them," Callie replied, "but not all. The other team also logs in laptops and both teams work on them as we get to them."

"So, you don't have any idea whose laptop Megan was working on?"

Callie shook her head. "No, not really."

Saligram also shook his head in negation.

I had a bright idea. "If you pull the laptops by ticket number, wouldn't the ticket tell you whose laptop was being worked on?"

It was Callie who answered. "Normally, yes. But you see, when L.P. came sniffing around the other day, we checked the tickets. Megan had one active ticket for a laptop belonging to some administrative assistant in Marketing. We couldn't find it. All the other laptop tickets in her queue were in the bins they were supposed to be in. None of those were missing."

"So, the missing laptop belongs to a secretary in Marketing?"

"Sort of," Callie replied. "You see, it was a new setup, a brand-new system. The admin had never touched it."

I raised an eyebrow. "There was nothing special about it?"

"Nothing other than being brand-new."

"You think somebody swiped it because they wanted a new computer?"

"Maybe," Callie said, "but it would have been easier to grab one off the loading dock. They have a whole pallet of them down there and in an area that doesn't have great coverage from security cameras."

"A puzzle, for sure," I mused.

"Yeah," Saligram added. "It didn't make sense to us, either."

I decided I had gathered everything I could from Megan's coworkers. "Thanks for taking a few minutes to talk. I'll let you guys get back to work now."

"Sure," Saligram said.

"No problem," Callie added.

I was frustrated. Despite talking with the two people who had worked with Megan on the last day of her life, I had learned little of value. According to the ticketing system, the only missing laptop other than Megan's as a new one waiting to be set up. It was barely possible that someone had taken it because they wanted a new laptop, but that seemed like too much of a coincidence. Why steal a laptop Megan was working on right before someone killed her? It didn't make sense.

I tried to think of a satisfactory theory to explain why a new laptop would be missing but failed to come up with one. It just *couldn't* be a coincidence. Or could it?

CHAPTER 24

Wednesday afternoon, I left work before my usual time, around three o'clock, and took Champ out for an early walk. Today his tail did the on-deck batter motion. We were on our way back to the condo when we passed one of the few remaining newspaper vending machines in Columbus. The *Dispatch* shared space with a variety of other specialty publications, including some that were almost entirely advertising. Out of the corner of my eye, I saw a headline that caught my attention:

Cops Re-Arrest Simmons's Ex-Boyfriend

I fumbled in my pockets, but I couldn't find any change for the machine. I ended up taking Champ back to the condo and racing over to a nearby convenience store to buy a paper there. According to the story, police had re-arrested Liam Murphy late the previous afternoon based on an anonymous tip. Reading further, though I discovered that little had come of this since they had released him shortly before midnight.

I checked the time. It was a quarter to five. I suspected that Murphy would be occupying a stool at Manny's by the time I could get there. I thought about texting Jenna but decided I would be back before her shift at the hospital ended. I didn't want to get the Mustang out again, so I ordered a Lyft and soon found myself in front of Manny's.

It was a little earlier that it was when I made my previous visit and the place had fewer customers. Ms. Nondescript was still behind the bar. Maybe she always was. Today she wore a Tom Petty T-shirt, exposing a full-sleeve tattoo on her left arm. Sitting on a stool at the bar was the redheaded giant, Liam Murphy. His clothes were like what he wore the last time I saw him, except this time it was an Ohio State sweatshirt. He drained the last of his can of PBR just as I walked in, which gave me my opening. I glided over to a stool next to him and ordered two beers, Pabst in the can for Murphy and a draft Budweiser for me.

"Good afternoon, Mr. Murphy," I opened cheerfully.

He turned and green eyes glowered at me. "*You* again?" I sensed Murphy didn't like seeing me.

"I hope to make this as painless as possible, Mr. Murphy."

"Ever time I turn around, somebody's askin' me a bunch a' fuckin' questions. Whadda *you* want?"

It was not an auspicious beginning. "I got you a beer, Liam," I said. For the first time, he noticed the can in front of him was full, not empty. His expression softened a little and I pressed on. "I understand the police took you into custody again yesterday?"

"Fuckers! I done tole 'em everything I know, and they yank my ass back downtown on accounta' some S.O.B that wouldn't even say who he was. Claimed he wanted to remain whatcha call, *anonymous*."

"I'm sure that was frustrating. Did the police tell you what this anonymous caller said?"

"Yeah, said I was th' one that offed Megan and if they'd sweat me real hard, I'd confess."

"I take it you didn't?"

Murphy looked indignant. "Hell, no! I didn't do nuthin so I ain't confessin' to nuthin'. That Eye-talian cop, Tosca, he did everything but stomp on my nuts, but I tole him to go pound sand."

I chuckled silently to myself imagining Tosca's reaction to that. "So, I gather it wasn't a very productive session for the detectives?"

"I tole 'em I already said what I had to say and there weren't no more. I think Tosca woulda kept me in th' poke if it hadn't a' been for that Black chick."

"Vickers?"

"Yeah, Vickers."

I took a drink of Budweiser. "Liam, you ever hear of the term 'stalking horse'?"

'Stalking horse' has a couple of definitions. In its more literal sense, it refers to a horse or something that looks like a horse that a hunter hides behind as he stalks game. The stalking horse allows him to do this without alarming the quarry. The term can also refer to something used to mask something like a motive or an action. I was beginning to get the impression that somebody had picked Murphy for the latter role.

When he said he hadn't heard of a stalking horse, I explained briefly, then continued, "You see, Liam, I think somebody is using you as a stalking horse. There's a killer out there looking for somebody to mask what he's doing, and I think, my friend, he's picked *you* to be that mask, to be his stalking horse."

Murphy wasn't much of a thinker, but the wheels were turning now.

I went on, "You see, he phoned in that bogus 'tip' to try to get the cops focused on you instead of him. That must mean he feels they're close to discovering him. I'm guessing, though, it didn't work since the detectives let you go in pretty short order."

"I wouldn't tell 'em nuthin' and they didn't have nuthin' more on me than they did th' last time, so they cut me loose."

Murphy's beer can was empty, so I ordered him another Blue Ribbon.

"They didn't even keep you overnight. I think they were just throwing something against the wall to see if it would stick. When it didn't, they released you."

"Helluva note," Murphy grumped, "when some asshole can call th' cops and *anonymously* have a body tossed in the poke." His voice dripped with contempt as he dragged out the word, "anonymously."

"Yes, it is Liam. Like I said, I think somebody tried to use you as a stalking horse *and it didn't work.*"

His face brightened a little as he realized that the attempt to suck him back into the case had been largely unsuccessful.

I finished my beer and ordered another. Murphy had already downed the new can, so I ordered one for him, too. Ms. Nondescript served them without a word.

I tacked in a new direction. "There's something else I'm interested in, Liam. Did Megan have a laptop in the apartment? Did you ever *see* a laptop, or did she ever *talk* about a laptop?"

"Sure," he replied. "She was in th' computer biz, ya know, so she always had a laptop. Carried it in that backpack of hers."

"Would you know if she ever had more than one laptop?"

"Not really. All looked th' same to me."

"And she never talked about her laptop or any other laptop?"

"Nah, we never talked about her work stuff."

This was disappointing. I'd hoped to get some clue as to whether Megan had been in possession of the laptop that Loss Prevention was now searching for.

Murphy took a drink from his can of Pabst. "Megan, she was real smart," he said, admiringly. "She'd start talking about that computer stuff and she'd lose me, like quick. So, we never talked about it much."

"That's all right," I said, though not feeling it.

"Ya think th' cops ever gonna figure out who killed her?"

"I know it doesn't look like it now, Liam, but I think they will," I told him, telling myself, Thinking: *And I'm going to help them.*

"Whole thing makes me feel real bad, ya know? I'm real sorry th' way things ended up with her and me."

For a minute, I though the redheaded giant was going to cry. Maybe there was more depth of emotion to him than I realized. Or maybe he was just a weepy drunk. Either way, I figured I'd extracted all the information I could from Mr. Liam Murphy. I laid two twenties on the bar and walked outside to order the Lyft that would take me back home.

CHAPTER 25

Jenna was still in her scrubs when she tapped at my door. Today, she had pulled her hair back in the loose ponytail she normally wore when she worked. I gently kissed her and welcomed her in. Champ added his welcome by licking her hand and swinging his tail from side to side. *Batter up!* I thought.

I filled her in on my latest and less than productive interview with Liam Murphy. She listened attentively and seemed as disappointed as I was that out meeting had not been more helpful.

"I feel like I'm going around in circles," I said. "I thought surely Murphy would know something about that laptop, or those laptops, whichever it is. And the videos didn't give a single solid clue as to who the Mystery Man might be. They're not talking to me, of course, but I get the impression that Vickers and Tosca aren't making much headway either. If they were, I don't think they would have bitten on that anonymous tip gag."

Jenna smiled sympathetically without saying anything. She knew I was venting and besides, there wasn't much for her to say.

I threw myself back on the sofa and closed my eyes. Jenna moved over next to me and began gently stroking my forehead and my temples. It was very relaxing. I enjoyed her soothing touch for several minutes, sitting up only to keep myself from going to sleep.

"Jenna, remember I told you the other day my daughter wants to meet you. How do you feel about that?"

She looked at me quizzically. "You did say that. She really does?"

I recounted my lunch with Heather for her. I thought she might not like the fact that I'd shared intimate details with my daughter, but it seemed to amuse her.

"Did you tell her about the bathrobe?" Jenna asked?

"Yes, I did."

She blushed slightly. "She must think I'm a dreadful tramp, then."

"She got a kick out of it. I think she admired you for going after something you wanted."

"She sounds like quite a girl. Tell me more about her," she said. "She knows quite a bit about *me*, I'd like to know about *her*."

"She *is* quite a girl. Heather is my baby. She's twenty-four, a paralegal, and is saving up money for law school. She is incredibly focused. She pursues her goals with determination and can be assertive without being aggressive. She's dating an attorney in the office, Doug Lewis, who, by the way, has the Dad Seal of Approval."

The last remark elicited a throaty laugh.

"Heather looks remarkably like her mother did at that age, except her hair is lighter and she has hazel eyes where Lisa's eyes were brown. I can't look at her without thinking about Lisa, but in a good way, not a sad way."

"Ben never wanted children," Jenna mused, "and early in our marriage, I was focused on establishing myself in my career. Later, our relationship was such that having children didn't seem like a good idea. I'm not sure I'd've made a good mother. I think I focused too much on nursing."

"Is that regret I'm hearing?"

"No, not exactly regret. I made a choice and I'm happy enough with it. I just sometimes wonder how things would have turned out if I'd made a different choice.

"I think you'd have made a fabulous mother. You're loving, generous, gentle, all qualities that mothers need."

Abruptly, she asked, "Does Heather approve of me? Of us?"

I thought for a quick minute, then answered, "I'm sure she does. I think the reason she wants to meet you is to see how closely you match her mental picture of you."

"No pressure, then," she giggled.

"There really isn't. Heather is a sweet girl and one of the least judgmental people I know. She got that from her mother. I was a little reluctant to bring this up right now, you know, so soon, but Heather was quite insistent. I told you she was determined!"

"I'd love to meet her. Don't you have a son, too?"

"Yes, David. He's 28, four years older than Heather, married, and lives in Chicago."

"Well, I want to meet him someday, too."

"If we don't get together before then, I'll take you up for a Cubs game in the spring."

"Baseball?"

"Yes. I've been a Cubs fan for years, decades, really."

"I don't know a lot about baseball, but it sounds like fun."

"I'll teach you everything you need to know," I promised. I loved seeing baseball at the ballpark. Having Jenna with me would be delightful. Only five more months before opening day.

Jenna rose to go. "If I don't get some clothes washed tonight, I'm going to have to go to work naked," she said.

I smiled at the thought of her naked as I stood up and kissed her lightly on the lips. "See you," I said.

She responded by pulling me close for a long, deep kiss, then gave a quick wave as she went out, closing the door behind her.

CHAPTER 26

On Thursday, I found I was able to put in almost a full, productive day at work. Brad still hovered over me a bit, but I think even he was surprised to see my work output return to its former level. I was in the office extra early that morning because I planned to leave early. Another perk of working for Brad was that he was not a stickler about office hours. If you were in the office for a decent portion of the day and got your work done, you could start and finish as it suited you. The only possible monkey wrench in my plans was Brad's weekly team meeting, which could sometimes drag on for a couple of hours. Normally, Brad has these meetings Friday afternoons, but this week, he rescheduled for Thursday. But Brad frequently cancels them at the last minute, too, and to my delight, he canceled the one scheduled for today before lunchtime.

Shortly after two, I locked my computer screens and headed out the door. I had special plans tonight, even though tomorrow would be a workday for me. Jenna and I had been too busy and too tired to have a real date earlier in the week, so we planned to make up for it tonight. I had promised to make dinner for her. My repertoire was rather limited, but what I could make was usually well-received. I decided to make a roast pork loin using a recipe I got from Heather. I had bought the roast a couple of weeks earlier and frozen it. All I had to do was pull it out of the freezer. I thawed it yesterday and it had been marinating all day today. I did need a few extras to accompany the main course, not least of which would be a couple of bottles of a good Côtes du Rhône. I liked the way things turned out the first time I shared a Côtes du Rhône with Jenna. Why change now?

I used my monthly pass to run my car through the carwash on Fifth Avenue before trekking over to the Giant Eagle on Third. Most of the time I enjoy grocery shopping for its own sake and take my time roaming the aisles. Today though, I was on a mission. I selected two bottles of Côtes du Rhône, two of Chandon, and a couple of California cabs. Six bottles earned me the half-case discount. As usual, I had to wait at the self-checkout until some came to verify my age. If I thought I *looked* under 21, it would be a complement, but since I know I don't, it's an annoyance. Assistance came promptly today, though, in the shape of a young woman with lime-green hair. She looked like a teenager but would have had to be at least 21 to process the sale of alcohol. I was on my way before I could fully work out a satisfactory answer to why anyone would want lime-green hair.

I pushed my shopping cart out to the parking lot to where I had left the Mustang. I won't say I'm absent-minded, but now and then it takes me a while to remember where I parked. Today, I found it without delay and opened the trunk to put the groceries in. I stopped cold.

Let me first say that I keep my car exceptionally clean, inside and out. My trunk is fastidious as well. The only thing I keep in the trunk permanently is the spare tire and an ice scraper. Now, as I peered into the Mustang's cramped luggage space, I saw a laptop bag lying on the trunk's carpet. And the laptop bag had something in it, apparently a laptop computer. I stared in surprise, trying to think of how it could have gotten there.

I stared at the bag for a minute in frowning concentration.

Then it hit me. It had to be Megan! The morning of that last Friday, Megan came down from her third-floor work area and borrowed my car keys. She said she'd left her phone in my car, but now I wondered if that wasn't just a ruse to get my car keys and stash the laptop in the Mustang's trunk. Since she didn't ask for the bag when I dropped her off, I suspected she had intended to hide it there. Then somebody killed her Friday night and she never had the opportunity to retrieve it. While that didn't bring me any closer to *why* she wanted to hide the bag in my trunk, I was satisfied that it answered the *how*. I dismissed the idea that she *wasn't* trying to conceal it; no other scenario made sense. On the other hand, remembering my conversation with Callie and Saligram, I couldn't begin to explain why she would want to hide a new laptop with nothing on it.

Why the hell would Megan want to stash a laptop in the trunk of my car and why was Detective Tosca so eager to find it?

I really wanted to examine the laptop and, more importantly, what was on it but decided doing that before I turned it over to the police would be completely foolish. The bag was a canvas-like material that didn't look like it would take prints, but the evidence technicians might be able to get prints off the zipper pulls or some of the other smoother surfaces. As for the laptop itself, its myriad smooth surfaces could be a gold mine for the fingerprint technicians, assuming someone hadn't wiped it clean. But even if I could manage to avoid leaving my own prints, I would probably damage or obliterate others that might be there. And waiting a few days to root around the laptop's hard drive before turning it over to Vickers and Tosca was out of the question. I'd have to give it to them as is. I wasn't happy about it but facing a charge of suppressing or tampering with evidence was not an appealing prospect, either.

Now I was in a dilemma. I'm sure the detectives, Tosca especially, would want—no, expect—me to call them right away with my discovery. My first thought was to do just that. But then I realized that getting involved with detectives and, probably, evidence technicians would put a serious dent in the evening I had planned with Jenna if it didn't wreck my plans altogether. I had a date tonight that I didn't intend to miss, detectives be damned. Tosca would squawk, but he was going to have to wait a little while anyway.

For a grocery store, Giant Eagle has an extensive wine selection in addition to housing a State Liquor Store. They helpfully provide complementary wine caddies for their shoppers. The caddies come as flat cardboard contraptions that easily fold out into a carton with space for six wine bottles. They are a little like the soft drink cartons we used to get when I was a boy, only for bigger bottles. The caddy gave me a perfect impromptu tool for moving the bag without leaving or damaging prints. I used the side of the caddy to gently push the laptop bag out of the way. I had finished loading my groceries before I realized that I should have simply put the groceries and wine in my back seat. Tosca probably wouldn't be happy about that, either, but it was too late. Checking to make sure I didn't have anything in the trunk that might spill, I closed the trunk lid, got in, and pointed the Mustang toward home.

CHAPTER 27

Jenna was as alluring as ever when I opened the door for her. Her honey blonde hair spilled over a red top that matched quite well with navy blue slacks. I told her she didn't need to bring anything but herself and she had taken me at my word. Champ meandered over, sniffed her proffered hand, and expressed his approval with his thick tail. Tonight, it was the helicopter again. She patted his head, and, to Champ's and my complete surprise, she produced a dog treat as if from thin air and offered it to him. David Copperfield couldn't have done it any smoother. Champ accepted the treat and quickly gulped it down.

"The way to a man's heart is through his stomach," Jenna laughed with her impish grin in evidence, "even if the man is a dog."

I laughed in response.

Since this was Jenna's first official visit to my condo, not counting the other night's pop-in, I gave her the grand tour. My place is small and functional. It is not swankily decorated, but neither is it bare and spartan. The entrance foyer opens into a combined living and eating space. Two bedrooms open off the right side, one of which I have fixed up as my home office. Tucked off in a corner is a smallish but well-appointed kitchen. Another corner is home to my modest wine collection.

In the bedroom, Jenna noticed a framed photograph on the nightstand and asked, "Is that Lisa?" The picture was one of our wedding photos and showed Lisa by herself in her wedding dress. I thought I had looked sharp that day in my pearl-gray tuxedo, but Lisa, beautiful Lisa, drew everyone's attention and hardly anyone had noticed me.

"Yes," I replied. "One of the pictures from our wedding."

"She was very beautiful." From the way she admired the picture, I could tell she meant it.

"She was every bit as beautiful inside as outside."

"Any wedding pictures of you?"

"Sure, somewhere. None that I thought could compare to that one." Jenna rewarded me with one of her smiles.

She put the picture back on the nightstand, almost reverently. I invited her to make herself comfortable on the sofa while I poured two glasses of Côtes du Rhône that I had decanted earlier. I sat down beside her and gently wrapped my left arm around her shoulders. She smiled.

"Dinner will be ready soon," I announced.

"Good," she said. "I'm starved. I missed lunch today."

Before long, everything *was* ready. Jenna moved to the table and I served. The menu consisted of roast pork loin with garlic mashed potatoes and asparagus. Heather's pork roast recipe was divine, and Jenna loved it, too. Wine snobs will tell you that you should serve white wine with pork, but Jenna and I agreed that the Côtes du Rhône complemented the roast nicely. I distracted Champ by cutting up some leftover steak from the refrigerator to top off his dog food.

We ate like the hungry people we were, with relatively little conversation, each reveling in the company of the other without feeling the need to break the silence. I cheated a bit on dessert, which was simply vanilla ice cream. Jenna didn't mind.

After we finished eating, Jenna sipped another glass of Côtes du Rhône while I cleared the table and loaded the dishwasher. I didn't start it, though, because it's a noisy dishwasher, and I wanted to watch the movie I'd selected for the evening. The dishes could wait until tomorrow.

As I loaded dishes, I reflected on the comfortable domesticity of the scene. Jenna was perfectly at home on my sofa and was well on her way to ingratiating herself with my dog. Anyone peeking in through a window would have assumed that we were a close couple of long standing. I liked the idea; it gave me a peaceful inner warmth. I had trouble putting it into words, but I took comfort from it, nonetheless.

Neither of us had seen a movie recently, so we decided we would watch one tonight. I have a small collection of DVD and Blu-Ray disks, plus subscriptions to a few streaming services. I found out that Jenna liked watching old Humphrey Bogart movies almost as much as I did. *The Maltese Falcon* and *The Enforcer* didn't fit tonight's mood, and neither did *The Big Sleep* or *Key Largo* despite their romantic subplots. I decided on *Casablanca* and loaded the disc into the player.

I joined Jenna on the sofa and snuggled up next to her. I knew all the scenes and much of the dialog by heart and, it turned out, so did Jenna. We watched enthralled, nonetheless. We brooded with Rick as he drank himself half blind waiting for Ilsa. We thrilled as Victor Laslo directed the orchestra in *Les Marseilles*, then laughed as Renault demanded his winnings after closing the café for having gambling. And, of course, we smiled approvingly at Renault's dramatic order to his subordinates to round up the usual suspects.

By the time Rick sent Ilsa off to catch the plane with Laslo, Jenna and I were making out on the sofa. Rick and Louie may have been beginning a beautiful friendship, but another beautiful friendship was blooming right here in my living room.

CHAPTER 28

As I predicted, Detective Tosca was not happy. I left messages for both him and Detective Vickers but, my luck, he'd been the first one to call back.

"Let me get this straight, West," he barked. "You found this *key* evidence *yesterday* afternoon and you waited until *this morning* to get around to calling?"

I held the phone away from my ear for a moment, then said, "I'm sorry, detective. I didn't know it was key evidence. *You* don't know it's key evidence." Almost instantly, I realized that that had been a mistake.

"Look here, West, we know you're running around trying to play detective on this thing and we've let you do it because we don't have time for your shit and, up to now, you haven't got in the way. *This* is getting in the way. I could run you in for concealing and tampering with evidence and, dammit, I will if you don't hand over that laptop bag *right fucking now!*"

I let that hang for a few beats before responding. "That's what I called you and Detective Vickers for, sir. I have the laptop bag, it's in the trunk of my car, I haven't touched it, and I called you to come get it."

"You stay right there, dammit. I'll have an evidence tech over before you can scratch your ass and *I'll* be over as soon as I can get free here. I got a *bunch* more questions for *you.*"

Marvelous. I fired off a quick email to Brad explaining that the police needed to talk to me again and that I wouldn't be in to work. I said "talk" because it sounded less sinister than "question."

Just how I wanted to spend my Friday, I thought. Good thing I'd taken Champ out before calling police headquarters because it looked like I was going to be stuck here for a while.

It wasn't quite as quick as Tosca had predicted, but within ten minutes there was a knock at my door. It proved to be the evidence technician Tosca promised. She was a young woman, probably in her late twenties, with frizzy-looking brown hair pulled back in a tight ponytail. She introduced herself as Francine Welty and I led her down to my space in the garage, where I pointed to the Mustang. She opened the large duffel bag she carried with her, then pulled out and donned a white moon suit along with latex gloves. That wasn't a good sign. I deduced it meant she wasn't going to just take the laptop bag and go. Moments later, she proved me right.

She started by dusting the trunk of the car for fingerprints, being especially careful around the latch and keyhole. When I told her that I'd washed the car just before I discovered the laptop, she was unfazed and kept on dusting. Every time she found something that looked like it might be a fingerprint, she photographed it in place, then carefully lifted it with adhesive tape and gently placed the tape on a white card, each time making notes on the back of the card.

I'd have to wash the car again. Probably more than once.

When she finally opened the trunk, she extracted the laptop bag, which she carefully placed in a clear plastic evidence bag and then sealed it.

"That it?" I asked, hopefully.

"No, sir. I've got to examine the interior of the trunk itself."

Marvelous.

For the next two hours, Ms. Welty went through the Mustang's trunk as if she expected to find gold nuggets hidden under the carpeting. First, she took a small vacuum from her bag and ran it all over the interior of the trunk, then dumped what it had slurped up into another evidence bag and tagged it. She repeated the process, only this time with adhesive tape, carefully examining each strip and, more often than not, pulling something off the tape with a pair of delicate tweezers, dropping it into yet another evidence bag which she also tagged.

Next, she pulled out the carpet itself and repeated the entire process on the underside of the carpet and the metal floor of the trunk. Finally, almost as an afterthought, she dusted the metal surfaces on the inside of the trunk lid for fingerprints. No automated carwash was going to get rid of the stubborn black powder on the *inside* of the trunk. I don't know about Ms. Welty, but by the time she finished, *I* was exhausted. I also marveled at the amount of stuff she pulled out of that duffel bag. Mary Poppins would have been jealous.

Ms. Welty had begun packing up when my phone rang. I groaned when I saw it was Tosca's number, then answered, "Yes, detective?"

"I told you to stay put. Where the hell are you?"

"I'm in the garage with your evidence technician. She's finishing up. I'll be up in about five minutes."

Tosca emitted a grunt of dissatisfaction and hung up without saying anything else. I bade Ms. Welty good day and rode the elevator up to the tenth floor to meet the dyspeptic detective.

Tosca skipped the small talk. "I want to know why you hung onto that laptop overnight."

That again. "Detective, I had plans last night and I didn't think one evening was going to make much difference."

Detective Tosca was not mollified. "That's *my* judgment call, not yours."

"I'll concede that," I said. "What else?" I doubted he made an in-person visit to ask me what he'd already asked over the phone.

"Can we go inside?"

He probably wanted to eyeball my place without the formality of a search warrant. Since I didn't feel I had anything to hide, I agreed. "Sure, come on in," I said, unlocking the door.

Champ greeted us warily. No antics with the tail until he decided this stranger was okay. Giving the dog a pat on the head, I led the way to the living space where we each picked a chair on opposite sides of a low glass table. The detective and I exuded all the warmth of two hockey teams facing off.

"I'm curious," the detective started, "how you ended up with this laptop and why you didn't tell us about it before."

"The last one is fairly simple," I replied truthfully. "I didn't mention it because I didn't know I had it."

"I find that hard to believe." Always the skeptic, Tosca.

"Whether you believe it or not, it's the truth. I didn't know the bag was in my trunk until I opened it yesterday afternoon to load groceries."

"You should have called us right then," he admonished.

"We've covered that. I promise to do better next time."

Tosca's eyes narrowed, studying my face to see if he could detect a hint of sarcasm. I put on my best innocent look and continued, "I was careful not to touch the laptop bag, even though I doubt you'll get any prints off it. Most of it is made of something like canvas." I didn't mention that I'd loaded my groceries in the trunk with the bag.

"You never know what those lab guys can do," he said. I thought I heard a note of respect in his voice. Then he scowled and said, "You never told me how it got in your trunk."

"There we enter the realm of speculation. I don't actually *know* how it got there, but I have a surmise."

"Let's hear it."

"That last morning Friday before she was killed, Megan came down to my office and asked to borrow my car keys. Said she'd left her phone in my car. She wasn't a person who forgot things, but it *could* have happened that way. Anyway, I let her have the keys. The only thing I can figure is that she put the laptop in the trunk then. I'm not sure why, but my best guess is that she wanted to hide it."

"So, it's her laptop?" Tosca's tone became less confrontational and more thoughtful.

"Not necessarily." I explained about the two missing laptops. "So, you see, it could be hers, it could be the one missing from Desktop Support, or it could be a different laptop altogether."

The detective thought that over. "We should be able to tell that as soon as the forensic computer guys get their hands on it," he said.

"Maybe. Then again, maybe not. Did you know that we encrypt the boot drives on all our company laptops? At least they're *supposed* to be encrypted."

He didn't look pleased. "I don't know anything about that computer stuff but the guys in the lab are pretty good."

They might be, I thought, but we'd see how they made out trying to crack the military-grade encryption algorithms we used at CIS.

"And another thing," I continued. "According to a couple of techs I talked to in Desktop Support, this missing laptop was supposed to be brand new, waiting to be set up. So, even if you *do* break the encryption, you might come up empty.

"Now, I suppose you'll keep the laptop as evidence, but I know your lab won't mess with the original disk, they'll make a bit-for-bit copy before they start trying to examine it. If they can't get past the encryption and you give me one of the copies, I *might* be able to help out."

Tosca looked skeptical. "How's that?"

"I've been in IT for more than thirty years, and I've learned a thing or two." I didn't tell him that Megan had shared a few tricks they use in Desktop Support with me.

"I'll keep that in mind." The detective stood up and walked toward the door. Over his shoulder, he fired a parting shot. "Don't play any more games with us, West," he said as he banged out the door.

CHAPTER 29

When I told Jenna about Megan's two cats, Smoke and Mimosa, needing a new home. she agreed to adopt them. I called Megan's brother, Carl at the dealership where he worked and arranged to pick up his unwelcome feline guests. I drove to his house after my encounter with Detective Tosca to get them. The cats' attitudes during the ride downtown was chilly at best; at times they were downright hostile. Now they warily explored their new environment while displaying stereotypical feline indifference. Jenna had made space for a litter box in her spare bathroom and put out food and water just outside the kitchen. Both animals sniffed at the food bowl briefly and continued exploring their new digs.

"Maybe I should have gone with canned food instead of dry," Jenna mused.

"I'll bet when they get hungry enough, they'll eat whatever you put out." Eventually the cats proved me right.

Smoke was completely gray from end to end. Even her nose was gray, a shade darker than her short fur. "Smoke" was a name that fit her well. Wending her way through the condo, she even reminded me of a drifting cloud of smoke and her yellow eyes evoked fire

Mimosa, on the other hand, had long, fluffy orange fur, green eyes, and a pink nose. Tiny streaks and spots of white highlighted her coat. While it was easy to determine the origin of Smoke's name, I was at a loss to explain how Megan had come up with "Mimosa" for an orange cat. Maybe she drank a mimosa after bringing her home, maybe she found her under a mimosa tree, or maybe she picked the name out of a dictionary. It was pointless to try to figure it out.

From the very first time I met Jenna, I was aware that she frequently had a smile playing at her lips. I liked that about her. I saw that smile now as she watched the two cats, not quite sure of themselves, gingerly stepping around her living room. "They look like they dropped in from another planet," she said, "and are trying to figure out where they are and how they got there."

"You're probably not too far of the mark. I gather their universe with Carl was pretty constrained."

"Should we introduce them to Champ," she asked?

"Oh, sure, after they've had a few days to settle in."

Jenna agreed that was a good idea and busied herself making dinner. We had been alternating preparing meals for each other for our date nights, and today it was her turn. She was a wizard in the kitchen and everything that came out of it was both appealing and delicious. I, on the other hand, was merely a competent cook with a limited repertoire. I could make edible food, but I was light years behind Jenna in culinary skill and finesse. I didn't ask what she was making since she liked that to be a surprise. Instead, I busied myself shaking two martinis. A nice cocktail before dinner and a good wine with it would elevate the enjoyment of the evening.

"I had a lovely encounter with Detective Tosca this morning," I said. I related the visits of Ms. Welty and the grouchy detective.

"Why in the world do you think Megan would put her laptop in your trunk?" she mused.

"Well, for one thing, I'm not certain it's *her* laptop. It could be one that somebody sent to Desktop Support to work on or it could be a brand new one waiting to be set up."

"Do you think she was hiding it, or did she just want to make sure she didn't forget it."

The latter had occurred to me, but I dismissed it. If she simply wanted to transport the laptop, she wouldn't have needed to put it in my trunk, nor would she have left it behind when I dropped her off. "I have a strong feeling she was hiding it," I said, "but as to why, I have no idea."

"Think it was tied in with her murder?"

"The cops sure think so, at least that's how I read Tosca this morning. He was really pissed that I didn't call him last night."

Jenna giggled at the mention of last night. A missing laptop had been the last thing on our minds. "I hope he got over it," she said.

"Maybe, I don't know. He sure thought it was her laptop, though. It *might* be, of course, but then again, it might not. He was intrigued by the possibility that it could be someone else's.

"The other thing," I continued, "is that the disk in that laptop is probably encrypted, in which case, the police might not be able to read what's on it. I'm not sure how good they are at breaking encryption. And then, even if they do break it, they might find a blank computer."

"So, even though the police now have the laptop, they still might not be able to tell anything from it?"

"Exactly. I can just imagine how *that* will make Tosca feel."

We sipped martinis while we talked about the case until Jenna announced that dinner was ready. Tonight, it was lasagna accompanied by a small salad and French bread, with tiramisu for dessert. Jenna made perfect lasagna and her tiramisu was top-notch. The cats found a place where they could watch us while we ate without us being able to easily observe them.

We began talking about food as we ate, then Jenna asked, "Is your daughter a good cook?

"She has some good recipes. That pork roast we had the other night was one of them. I think she and Doug like to cook together a lot."

"That sounds like fun, sort of, but I have my own ways in the kitchen, and I think I work better alone."

"Me too," I agreed.

"But trading off cooking is a nice way to share without getting in each other's hair," she continued. "Not everybody can share their kitchen space with another person."

"I totally agree. Back to your question, everything of Heather's that I've eaten has been yummy."

"I was thinking about what you said the other night, about Heather wanting to meet me. I want to meet her, too. Think she could do that this weekend?"

"I can ask."

During the rest of our dinner, we talked about our families, our childhoods, and a dozen other subjects. We specifically avoided talking any more about Megan.

CHAPTER 30

Heather was delighted to meet us for dinner Saturday and asked if she could bring Doug along. I told her of course, she could, and we set a date for 6:30 at Lindey's. Lindey's has been around for years and is one of the best spots in German Village, which is quite an accomplishment since there are several excellent restaurants in that neighborhood.

For the occasion, Jenna wore a green poncho with tan slacks, the poncho all but covering the white blouse she wore underneath. I went with my usual business casual that I wore in the office. The hostess seated us at a table for four in one of the dining areas in the back part of the restaurant. While we waited, I ordered a Bombay Sapphire martini while Jenna decided on a glass of Sauvignon Blanc. About ten minutes after our drinks arrived, I was devouring the second olive from my martini when I saw Heather and Doug approaching our table.

We stood and I made introductions. "Heather, Doug, this is my girlfriend, Jenna Stone." I subtly emphasized 'girlfriend.' "And Jenna, this is my daughter, Heather West and Doug Lewis." They all shook hands.

I could tell immediately that something was up. Heather's eyes danced with an excitement that she barely contained. After sitting, she placed her left hand ostentatiously in the middle of the table. She had a large diamond on her left ring finger.

"Daddy, we're engaged!" she exclaimed. "Doug asked me last night and I said yes!"

Jenna and I offered our congratulations and I said, "This most certainly calls for a toast!" I would come back to my cocktail later, but for now, I caught the server's eye and ordered a bottle of champagne for the table. While we waited, Jenna and I admired the engagement ring. Heather kept bubbling.

"Oh, I *so* wanted to call you last night, Daddy. But Doug thought it would be a nice surprise to tell you today when I could show you the ring. Besides, I didn't want to interrupt anything." She glanced briefly at Jenna who, just as briefly, blushed slightly. "Anyway," she giggled, "Doug had to hide my phone, so I didn't spill the beans prematurely."

Our server brought the champagne and poured four glasses. As the dad, I supposed it was my duty to propose the toast. "To Heather and Doug, long life and a happy marriage with many blessings."

We all clinked glasses and drank, then Heather surprised me. "To Daddy and Jenna, may they be happy together."

I smiled and felt warm inside, but I stole a glance at Jenna to see her reaction. I needn't have worried. She was smiling her most radiant smile. I relaxed and took a generous sip of the champagne.

"Daddy tells me that you two have become, well, close," Heather said to Jenna. She wasn't shy, that one. For her part, Jenna wasn't the least bit embarrassed and took up the conversation.

"Yes. He needed a little encouragement at first," she said, flashing her impish grin at me, "but I'd say we've become *quite* close."

Heather's eyes twinkled, knowing that by 'encouragement' Jenna was talking about the bathrobe on the floor. Then she took on a more serious look "You know, Daddy really likes you. I'm glad to see him with somebody. He had a hard time getting over Mom's death."

It's a funny feeling to hear people talking about you as though you weren't in the room.

"Your Daddy is quite special to *me*. I feel lucky to be with him."

Jenna recounted the story of her marriage to Benton Diehl, how it had unraveled, how that had left her empty and incomplete, and how she felt whole again. I found the interplay between the two women fascinating. Jenna was technically old enough to be Heather's mother, but she was also young enough that she could be a close girlfriend.

During dinner, Doug told us about some of the cases he was working on, at least the parts he could tell without betraying confidences. Then he looked at me and said, "Mr. West, uh, Dad—I guess I should call you Dad, huh?"

I laughed. "Dad is fine."

"Dad, Heather told me a little bit about that girl that was murdered. I think she said you knew her?"

"Yes, we worked at the same company and carpooled together. I was the one that found her, which earned me a few visits with the police. I can't seem to back off and let the cops deal with it."

Doug's face was a mixture of interest and concern. "Don't run afoul of the police. Think they're close to catching the guy?"

"I don't know, Doug. I hope so, but I don't know for sure. But what I *do* know is that this isn't a topic for *this* occasion."

During a long, leisurely dinner, Heather and Doug got to know Jenna and she got to know them. As we were making our way outside, Heather gave me a quick hug, bussed me on the cheek, and whispered, "Daddy, she's a gem. Hold on to her."

I smiled. "I know, honey. I'll do my best," I said.

Rather than drive, Jenna and I had taken Lyft to the restaurant and now we took another back. We held hands in the back seat. During the ride, she said softly, "Your daughter's amazing. You did a good job with her."

"Thank you, but her mother helped. A lot."

Back in our building, Jenna concentrated on selecting a bottle from my small wine "cellar" while I took Champ out for his evening constitutional. Today his tail kept switching between the helicopter and the baseball bat. By the time we were back inside, Jenna had poured two glasses of pinot noir. We enjoyed our wine and talked about the evening until it was time for bed. I was pleased that Jenna didn't object to Lisa's picture on my nightstand.

Later, as I drifted off to sleep, Jenna nuzzled my ear and whispered, "I love you, Greg."

Wow! This was a whole new ballgame.

CHAPTER 31

Jenna didn't mention the "L" word again during our leisurely breakfast Sunday morning. Since she had plans for the afternoon, she went back to her own condo after we finished eating. This gave me time to myself to think over last night. It sent tingles through my body to hear Jenna's "I love you," but I needed some time to process it and clarify my own thoughts before I had a serious talk with her about it.

The weather was cold almost every day now. The sun was shining brightly today but it was below freezing when I hooked up the leash and put on my Carhart to take Champ for an extended morning walk. We ambled north along High Street, past the convention center and the Cap and into the Short North. I had decided to take Champ up to Goodale Park despite the cold weather to give me a chance to sort out my feelings. My heavy coat helped keep me warm and I knew Champ wouldn't mind. Labradors are cold-weather water dogs. As we strolled, my brain went to work.

Love.

It had been more than four years since I'd heard Lisa tell me she loved me. I liked the idea, and my first reaction was to respond with, "I love you, too." But how does somebody know if they're *really* in love? Were Jenna and I in love or was it merely a physical attraction?

I thought back to the time when Lisa and I were dating. From the first time I saw the pretty brunette with the dimples and the winning smile, I was smitten. The physical attraction was immediate and obvious. As we dated and got to know each other, respect and admiration mingled with desire Lisa and I shared many interests and enjoyed spending time together. The more time we spent in each other's company, the more I realized that I wanted to spend the rest of my life with her. We shared goals and we shared dreams. That, I decided, was love.

I brought my thoughts back to the present. I had deep affection for Jenna and making love with her was about as close to heaven I expected to get in this life. The physical attraction was obviously there. She was smart, funny, found satisfaction in her career, and we enjoyed being together. I'd like to think that, someday, Jenna and I might share goals and dreams, that we'd have the kind of relationship I'd had with Lisa. And therein lay a problem.

Lisa had been everything to me when we were married. I cherished her when she was alive, and I cherished her memory now. But Lisa was gone, and now here was another woman who wanted to be part of my life. I wrestled with the same question I'd wrestled with when Jenna and I first slept together. As moronic as it sounded, I felt like I was dishonoring my late wife's memory by being with another woman. Would Lisa have wanted me to stay faithful to her memory, single and celibate? We'd never talked about it, but I didn't really think so, at least I *hoped* not. If the roles were reversed, I believe I would want her to move on. Dead people can't feel jealousy, after all.

A large COTA bus swooshed by, stirring a chilled wind in its wake that tugged at my otherwise warm coat.

If I loved Jenna, did that mean I loved Lisa less? And if I kept loving Lisa's memory, would that be fair to Jenna? The more I thought about it, the more I realized I was approaching this from the wrong direction. I was considering things as if I were involved with two women at the same time. Lisa had been real in the past. Jenna was real in the present. *Here I go again*, I thought, *seriously overthinking the situation*. I can't seem to break myself of that habit!

Another bus zoomed noisily by, trailing a miasma of noxious diesel exhaust.

Let's start again. I thought. Jenna was pretty, Jenna was sexy, Jenna was smart, and Jenna had said she loved me. Did she really mean that, or was it just pillow talk? Was it a sweet nothing whispered in a moment of passion, or did it reflect deeper feelings and emotions? From what I knew of Jenna, and I was learning more every day, she wasn't the kind of woman who would toss that phrase around lightly. She would say it because she meant it.

Now, what about sorting out my own feelings? My affection for Jenna was genuine, and there was no question that I found her attractive and desirable. Our physical relationship was everything I could want and more. We liked a lot of the same things but had enough divergent interests to keep us from boring each other. I enjoyed every minute I spent with her and, when we were apart, I eagerly anticipated the next time we could be together. We were equally comfortable quietly spending an evening at home as we were doing something adventurous. We were, in all respects, already a couple.

God! I sounded like a teenager!

Jenna and I had both tried marriage and learned that things didn't always turn out "happily ever after." My marriage had been almost deliriously happy, but it was torn apart when Lisa died. Jenna's had been, from all I gathered, somewhat empty before a philandering husband wrecked it completely. Maybe it was too early to worry about what "forever" might mean for Jenna and me. But I was now very, very certain that I wanted to be with her for the long haul. I could only hope that she felt the same way.

I think I had my answer. I *did* love Jenna!

"Champ," I said to the dog, "I *love* that woman. What do you think of *that?*" He slowly rotated his tail in approval.

That settled, it was time to go home. I gently turned Champ around and led him back toward our condo.

CHAPTER 32

Wednesday morning, I was in deep concentration planning some storage provisioning that Brad had asked me to do when my cell phone rang. I grimaced when I looked at caller ID and recognized Detective Tosca's number. "Good morning, Detective Tosca," I said in a slightly saccharine voice.

"Guess you were right. The lab couldn't break the encryption on that drive." In character, Tosca skipped all manner of greeting and dove right into business. "You still think you want to take a crack at it?"

I grinned to myself. Mister Macho Detective was now asking for *my* help. "Sure, I'll give it a whirl."

"Good. I'll send it right over. You at work now? You want it there or at home?"

"Yes, I'm at work and the office will be fine, detective." I was almost laughing now at Tosca's humbled attitude.

As an afterthought, he added, "We got a bunch of prints off the laptop itself. Some, on the outside, were the dead girl's, but there were a bunch we couldn't identify. Looks like maybe five or six different people handled it."

"I wouldn't be surprised. It *is* a company computer, after all. So, no matches at all?"

"No," the detective said unhappily. "I mean, we ran 'em through AFIS and the state database, but nothing hit."

"Again, not surprising. CIS tries not to hire felons, you know."

I thought I heard Tosca grin. "Anyway, the disk's on the way." He paused, then, "And thank you." Unexpected gratitude. *That* was different.

Approximately thirty minutes later, the front desk called to tell me that there was a policeman in the lobby who wanted to see me. Ambling down to the visitor's lobby I met a large uniformed officer, the spitting image of a beefy cop from Central Casting. He handed me a plastic bag containing the disk.

The bag containing the disk—a copy of the original, I was sure—was clear plastic. A large red bar ran across the top of it with the word "EVIDENCE" stenciled in large white letters. I maneuvered the bag so that the red bar was not visible. No need to excite curiosity or comment from my coworkers. If Tosca thought I was going to work on the disk immediately, though, he was mistaken. I had plenty of work that CIS was paying me to do and the disk would have to wait. Jenna worked today, too, and we didn't have plans for tonight. I'd have plenty of time to try to unlock the disk's secrets when I got home.

Back at my cubicle, I found Henry Ames and Rob Ford engaged in spirited conversation. The subject appeared to be video gaming, something I had little interest in. Both noticed the plastic bag with the disk in my hands.

"Whatcha got, man?" Rob inquired. Today he wore a Cleveland Browns sweatshirt with the jeans.

"It's a hard disk, dummy." Dumb questions deserve smart-ass answers.

"I can see *that* numb nuts. What's the deal with it?"

Looking down, I saw that my efforts to cover the "EVIDENCE" label were less than successful. "I'm doing a favor for Detective Tosca," I answered truthfully.

Now Henry seemed interested. "What kind of favor?" he asked.

"I don't think I'm supposed to talk about it. Maybe later but not now."

They accepted this glumly, their faces showing more curiosity than a roomful of cats as they went back to discussing the respective merits of different gaming systems. I locked the disk away in a cabinet and put it out of my mind by concentrating on some new tasks Brad had given me.

Later that afternoon, I happened to see Judson Battenslag striding through the office. He looked like a battleship running at flank speed: big, powerful, imposing. I marveled at his size. I guess I'd never really noticed his solid build before. I noticed now. He looked very much like the standout lineman he'd been in college, slightly taller than me, heavier, and more muscled. Could *he* have been the Mystery Man in the videos? Unlikely, but possible. Definitely possible.

Brad's task list proved to be more time-consuming than I expected. I had to reconfigure dozens of servers and modify their storage profiles. By lunchtime I discovered I was less than half done. Afternoon had started to turn into evening before I finished the last item and locked up to go home, making sure to retrieve Tosca's disk first. I wanted to see Jenna, but she was usually tired after twelve hours on the floor and often went to bed early, especially after her third day in a row of twelve-hour shifts. Tonight was going to be a good night to tackle the disk drive Tosca had sent me.

With sundown, the thermometer had dipped into the upper twenties. I donned my heavy Carhart to take Champ on his evening walk. Enthusiastic and as impervious to cold weather as usual, the big black dog trotted south down High Street with me in tow. At the Statehouse, we'd cut east on Broad when he suddenly decided in mid-block that he was ready to go home. We ambled up Pearl Street, which is more like an alley than a street at that point. We had almost reached Gay Street when two ear-splitting explosions boomed off the surrounding buildings. It took me a few moments to realize that what I'd heard were gunshots and, with the buildings that lined the street functioning as an echo chamber, I had no idea where they came from. A third shot might have lightly grazed my right cheek, or it might have been just the bullet's wake I felt, but it put the fear of God in me.

Champ either saw or sensed where the shots came from. He snatched the leash from my hand and took off like a cannonball back in the direction we'd come from, the leash trailing behind him. Two more reports, then a howl of pain. Champ stumbled, fell, and rolled a couple of times before coming to a stop. I looked up and caught a brief glimpse of a shadowy figure disappearing up Lynn Alley in the direction of Third Street. I grabbed my phone and dialed 9-1-1 as I ran toward Champ.

"9-1-1, what is your emergency?"

"A guy shot at me and then shot my dog." I was literally screaming at the phone.

"Please calm down, sir, so I can understand you. When and where did this happen?"

"I was on Pearl Street, near Gay. The guy with the gun was further south on Pearl,"

"Is the man with the gun still there."

"I don't know. I don't think so," I replied. "He booked east on Lynn Alley. If he's still there, I can't see him from here."

"And you are at Pearl and Gay?"

"I'm still on Pearl but about halfway between Lynn Alley and Gay Street."

"Officers are on the way."

In the distance, I heard a siren moan as I bent down over a motionless Champ. He wasn't dead, thank God, but he was whimpering and bleeding. My big black Labrador looked small and helpless lying there in the middle of the street. The siren grew louder and another one nearby joined it. Abruptly, the sirens stopped as two squad cars screeched to a halt on Gay Street. A uniformed officer debouched from each car. They both approached me, gun in one hand and a powerful flashlight held high in the other. I heard another siren stop nearby, probably at Third and Lynn, and soon saw another flashlight beam probing the darkness of Lynn Alley.

All three cops huddled around me and the motionless black form on the pavement. "We notified the detectives. They're on the way," the short one said.

Another officer, examining Champ, said, "The dog's not hurt too bad. I think he can make it if you get him to a vet."

Fat chance of that if the detective squad was going to grill me. Then I thought of Jenna. I quickly dialed her number and, when she answered, I spilled the story, words tripping over each other. "Jenn, some son-of-a-bitch just shot at me and shot Champ…"

Jenna interrupted. "Are *you* hurt? Did they shoot *you?*" Panic infused her voice.

"No, I'm fine, but Champ needs a vet right away and I can't get away to take him because I'm going to have to stay here and talk to the police."

"Where are you?" I told her and she said, "I'll be right there," and she hung up.

Within five minutes, she was there, her blue Prius driving slowly down Pearl Street. She jumped out of the car and gave me a hug that came close to squeezing the breath out of me. Then she knelt to look at Champ. She stroked his head and spoke softly to him, then she loaded him into the hatchback of her car and drove away. Champ is a big boy, close to eighty pounds, but Jenna lifted him as if he'd been a sack of feathers. Nurses have many hidden talents, I decided.

The officers had secured the crime scene, or at least what we presumed was the location of the shooter, by the time the detective arrived. Of course, it was Tosca.

"West," he said, "I shoulda known you'd be in the middle of this." He tried to sound tough, but was that genuine concern I saw in his eyes? "What happened here?"

"I wish I knew, detective. I was walking my dog minding my own business when this bastard took a shot at me. Three shots, in fact."

"You're sure there were three?"

"Pretty sure. The first two were close together, then one more that I thought might have grazed my cheek. You know, people always say when they hear gunshots that they think they are firecrackers? In this concrete canyon," I swept my hand in front of me indicating the expanse of Pearl Street, "it sounded like a couple of sticks of dynamite.

"My dog went after the guy lickety-split and he shot him."

"One shot?"

"No, two. I think it was the second one that hit him."

Tosca looked around, "Where's the dog now?"

"Jenna—that is, my neighbor—took him to the vet."

"Oh, so he was still alive?"

"Yes," I responded, "he was. I'm not sure how badly he was hurt. The lighting here doesn't lend itself to medical examinations."

Tosca nodded his agreement. "You get a look at the guy?"

"Not really. With all the echoes, I couldn't really tell where the shots came from. I only figured that out when Champ took off after him. By the time I looked in his direction, he was beating feet down Lynn toward Third."

"Swell spot for an ambush," Tosca mused. "Poor lighting to make identification difficult, multiple exit routes. He must think he's a damn good shot with a handgun, though, if it expected he could plunk you from that distance in the dark."

"Maybe," I said. "But then again, he missed me three times."

Tosca nodded agreement again and went over to talk to the evidence technician who was carefully examining the street, probably looking for shell casings. I noticed that it was not Ms. Welty but a youngish looking man with bushy black hair.

Tosca came back. "Kurt's already found a couple of shell casings, nine mil, and he's looking for the rest. If we can match the casings to a known gun, we might get somewhere, but I'll bet my pension we won't."

"No takers, detective."

CHAPTER 33

Jenna greeted me at the door with a bear hug that threatened to crush the breath out of me. I got a similar greeting last night after finishing with Tosca, leading me to conclude that she still hadn't processed the trauma completely. "How's Champ?" she asked when she finally let go.

"Champ is, well, Champ. He's doing fine, but between you and me, I think he's milking it for all its worth." That elicited a wan smile.

Champ was, in fact, doing well. The bullet hit him in the withers and penetrated muscle but no joints or vital organs. It had not lodged inside the dog's body, so there had been nothing for the vet to remove. She cleaned the wound and took a few stitches to help control the bleeding. She kept the dog overnight for observation but sent him home this morning with prescriptions for antibiotics and pain pills. Now the dog lay crashed out on the floor of my condo looking stoned and relaxed.

Jenna shut the door, then reached over and pulled me close for a slow, romantic kiss. We'd both had traumatic experiences although, if it were a contest, I think I was winning.

Tonight, we had Chinese take-out. Jenna dished out the food while I shook a couple of martinis. "I never thought of having martinis with Chinese food," she said.

"Didn't you know," I replied, grinning, "that martinis go with *everything?*" Frankly, I felt like I could use a good, stiff drink. Jenna probably could, too.

We ate mostly in silence. Both of us were exhausted and we were content to simply enjoy being close to each other. I had already decided to go back to my condo for the night. I needed to sleep, and I didn't want to leave Champ alone just yet. Jenna understood. Her eyes looked tired and I suspected she was going to crash early, too.

We kissed goodbye, a slow, sensuous kiss that held a promise of things to come.

Back in my own unit, I saw the disk drive, still in its evidence bag, where I had left it on the coffee table. In a way, I was eager to examine the drive and see if I could break the encryption. I was also dead tired and needed to sleep. The drive would have to wait for the weekend.

Hoping I wasn't running out of PTO, I sent Brad an email saying that I wouldn't be in again tomorrow but didn't explain why. Then I tumbled into bed and slept the sleep of the dead.

I should have tackled the disk when I got up Friday, but curious as I was, I couldn't muster the mental energy it would require. I decided to take Champ out for a long walk instead. The bullet that clipped him in the withers had done minimal serious damage. He was able to walk normally if he didn't run. The pain pills probably helped. Still, he gave me a quizzical look when I snapped the leash to his collar. It was uncomfortably close to the withers, so he was careful not to tug on the leash. His tail was virtually stationary, no helicopter or baseball bat today.

We took a short walk around the block, then another. By the end of the second circuit, he was walking more confidently. I hoped this was a sign of a quick recovery. Or maybe it was the pain pills.

Back in the condo, I again avoided the disk drive. Instead, I picked up my Kindle to catch up on some reading, returning to *The Accidental President*. I was surprised to learn that, although Truman had historically low approval ratings when he left office in 1953, in his first few months as President, he scored higher marks than Franklin Roosevelt ever had. I immersed myself in the problems he faced winding down World War II while the Cold War began to simmer.

I guess I fell asleep. When the phone rang, it was getting dark outside and the Kindle had shut off. When I answered, it was Detective Vickers on the line. "Mr. West, Detective Tosca asked me to call you," she said.

"Yes?"

"They found all five shell casings at the scene from last night, all nine-millimeter and all apparently from the same gun, a semi-automatic." I thought the semi-automatic part was obvious; a revolver wouldn't eject shell casings. But I didn't say that to Detective Vickers. She went on, "They also found a few bullet fragments near where the dog was shot but nothing usable."

"Not surprised," I muttered.

"We're trying to match the casings against known guns, but nothing's turned up so far."

"Detective, I appreciate the effort, but Tosca offered to bet his pension that you won't find a match and I'm on his side in this one."

I heard Vickers give off a soft chuckle. "You're probably right, Mr. West, but we're going to try anyway."

I mumbled my thanks and rang off.

Donning the Carhart, Champ and I headed out for another walk. There was more spring in his step than there had been earlier in the day and the thick black tail oscillated slowly from side to side. We cut the walk short, though, because the wind was icy and piercing, even with the heavy coat. We were soon back in the coziness of my condo.

I wanted to see Jenna, but she had planned a night out with some girlfriends, nurses from the hospital, and was out of pocket for the evening. I didn't mind. I just missed her. I'd decided that tomorrow I bring up the "L" word.

CHAPTER 34

I held a single red rose in my hand as I tapped on Jenna's door. I caught a brief glance of two cats scampering under some furniture as she let me in. Smoke and Mimosa were making themselves at home.

Jenna was wearing a fuzzy green sweater, appropriate for Ohio's inhospitable late-fall weather. She thanked me for the rose and put it in a tall, slender vase she produced from a kitchen cupboard. The vase looked like crystal.

Tonight, we were going out. "Ready if you are," she said.

"I am." I was already wearing the Carhart.

Jenna donned a coat and closed and locked her door. Since it was unpleasantly cold for a walk up to the Short North, we decided to take the C-Bus instead. It was cold waiting for the bus, too, but at least the bus stop sheltered us from the wind. After about ten minutes, the C-Bus rumbled to a stop, and we climbed aboard. As we bounced up High Street, I said to Jenna, "I imagine a buckboard wagon would only be slightly more uncomfortable." She laughed and squeezed my hand.

We exited the bus at Russell, then crossed the street to Lemongrass Fusion Bistro. Soon we were chatting over Pad Thai and Riesling.

I updated her on Champ. "Looks like Champ is going to be fine, I'm happy to say. He started a little gingerly yesterday but when I walked him today, he had a lot of spring back in his step. And he's done with the pain pills."

"That's great to hear." Jenna genuinely liked Champ. His wounding had shaken her, too. "Have the police got any idea who did the shooting?"

"No. Detective Vickers called me yesterday evening to tell me they found all the shell casings. All were from the same gun, but so far, no match to anything they have on file. She said they'd keep trying to find a match. Tosca's money, and mine too, is on that proving futile"

"It's so scary," she said. "Why in the hell would anyone be shooting at *you?*"

"Sweetheart, *that* is the $64,000 question. I mean, the guy popped a couple at Champ because Champ took off after him, but I can't even imagine why somebody would be taking pot shots at *me*. It's not like he was mugging me or anything, he was a block away, and there wasn't anybody else he could have been shooting at. I *had* to be the target but I'm damned if I know why."

Jenna shuddered. She refilled our wine glasses from the bottle before continuing. "Greg, I'm really worried."

"I'm not exactly unmoved myself."

"Should you carry a gun?"

Some people are scared to death of guns. I'm not one of them. I even own one. But I had no intention of packing a pistol. "I think that's a really bad idea. A wild west shootout is the last thing I want and besides, if the guy'd been a better shot, all the guns in the world wouldn't have helped. I think—hope—my best bet is to stay close to people and out of back alleys."

Jenna's gray-blue eyes looked worried. "That doesn't sound like much protection to me."

"Maybe not, but I don't merit Secret Service protection."

She smiled slightly at the idea, then said, "Still, I want to keep you safe."

"You'll get no argument from me," I replied, and I meant it.

We changed the subject. While we finished dinner and the bottle of Riesling, Jenna told me about her night out with the nurses. I only knew a couple of them and found it difficult to keep track of the players without a scorecard. I tried, though. From the sound of it, the evening had been a tonic for Jenna, a nice break away from the stresses of work and worrying about phantom gunmen. When we finished, I paid, and we caught a southbound C-Bus that dropped us near our building. We were soon inside, the elevator zooming us to the tenth floor.

I escorted Jenna to her door, and she invited me in, an invitation I readily accepted. I was pleased to note that the cats had not knocked over the vase; the red rose was still gracing the coffee table where Jenna had left it.

Jenna poured two glasses of a dessert wine and brought them over to the coffee table. Then she lay down on the sofa with her head in my lap and her feet over the arm. Now was my chance.

"Jenna," I began, "I heard what you whispered to me Saturday night." I thought she might have blushed slightly.

"Oh, that. Greg, I'm sorry if I rushed things—"

"No, absolutely not. You just gave me a lot to think about, that's all."

"And what did you conclude?" She was looking intently at my face, searching for clues, I suppose.

"I've told you that I've had a pretty rough four years. I had a long and happy marriage to Lisa and, frankly, I never thought I'd ever find anybody else. Then you came along."

"And?"

"And you were wonderful—*are* wonderful."

"But?" This woman was reading my mind.

"But I couldn't quite shake the feeling that by being with you I was betraying Lisa. I know, it sounds silly—"

"No, no," she interrupted. "It doesn't sound silly at all." A brief pause, then she continued slowly, "My marital experience was so different from yours that I have trouble imagining how you feel, but I *think* I understand, at least I'm trying to." This woman was priceless.

"I'm not sure I understand it completely myself, Jenna. But I did decide one thing."

"And that was?" She was looking at me intently again.

"I love you." There. I'd said it.

Jenna was quiet for a few minutes, then spoke softly. "I don't think I can tell you how much I wanted, no *ached*, to hear you say that Greg." She paused briefly. "I heard about how broken up you were when Lisa died."

"How's that?" I asked.

"I had a long talk with Tillie in the laundry room one day." Ah, Ms. Truax. Tillie is famous for knowing just about everything about just about everybody in the building. "I guess you moved in not long after the accident."

"That's right. David—my son—convinced me to sell the house and all its memories and find a place that was solely mine. I sold it and bought my unit here."

"Tillie told me what a fantastic marriage you and Lisa had and how you grieved so when you lost her. You know what else she told me?"

"I can't even guess."

"She told me that she thought you and I would be good together. After my experience, I knew I wanted someone completely different from Ben. The way Tillie described, you sounded like the kind of man I wanted to be with, thoughtful, engaged, and, well, loving. The more I got to know you, the more I decided Tillie was right. That's why I, well, you know…" She giggled, obviously thinking about the bathrobe incident.

She raised up slightly and I bent down and kissed her gently on the lips. We sat in silence for quite a long while. Some people might find silence awkward, but Jenna and I could sit in quiet communion without necessarily feeling the need to speak. Smoke padded quietly over and uttered a low meow before settling in one of the chairs across from us. Mimosa established her throne on the other chair. The scene radiated domesticity and I took comfort from it.

Eventually, Jenna sat up and took a sip of the wine that she had been ignoring, then she put both her arms around my shoulders and hugged me tightly. "Where do we go from here?" she asked. "Where do you *want* it to go?"

I didn't have a ready answer. "I'm not completely sure yet. I know that I *do* want to be with you, but I haven't worked out all the details. Maybe we *shouldn't* make too many plans while there's some bozo out there gunning for me."

Jenna shuddered. "I don't want to think about that, not tonight." I agreed and held her close.

"The only thing that makes any sense is that it's somehow related to Megan's death. He didn't come after me when I found her, so either he didn't know I was in the picture then or it has to do with something I learned later. I'm inclined to think it's number two."

"Sound's logical," she said.

"And there are only two things," I continued, "that I've come across since that Friday, the surveillance video and that disk drive. I didn't see anything on the videos worth killing me over, so it *has* to be the disk. And if it is, maybe that's why he killed Megan, because she had the laptop with that disk in it."

"What could be on a laptop that would make it worth killing a person and trying to kill another?"

"Damned if I know, but I'm sure as hell going to try to find out."

CHAPTER 35

I had moved my computer tower from the floor to my desk to make it easier to work on it. Its case was open, and I went spelunking around in its guts. The disk Tosca sent me was a typical three-terabyte SCSI drive with a SATA interface. Finding an extra power connection was no problem, but I had to poke around a bit through the maze of cables before finding an empty port where I could plug in the SATA data cable. I fired up the computer and was pleased to see that it recognized the drive immediately. However, the contents were invisible because of the encryption. I set the drive to read-only.

For years, the FBI and other agencies have been trying to coerce the makers of encryption solutions to include a "back door" for law enforcement. They cite the usual litany of concerns about bad guys and terrorists using encryption to mask their activities. Fortunately, this appeal has so far failed to bear fruit. Back doors, once they are available, are there for everybody to use and open a Pandora's box of potential abuse.

Private companies, on the other hand, operate in a different world. They use encryption to protect assets they own, not somebody's personal property. Just like the First Amendment, which prohibits *Congress* from impinging on your right of free speech but leaves companies free to apply restrictions to their employees, nothing bars private organizations from peeking at the encrypted devices they provide for their employees to use. Megan had told me some time back that Desktop Support had a bunch of back door passwords, and even gave me a list of them. A perfect illustration of the perils of back doors, by the way.

I pulled Megan's list out of a desk drawer and went to work. She'd told me that Desktop Support randomly picked the back-door passwords from a list of one hundred passwords. Worst case, I'd have to try all hundred before unlocking the disk. That is, *if* the disk came from a CIS laptop and *if* its encryption used a back-door password from one of the hundred.

First password: *TheA1batr0$$AroundMyNeck.*

It's common for passwords that use words or phrases to substitute numbers and symbols for letters. The job would be much easier if I could cut and paste the passwords. All I had was a paper list. Was that a lower-case el in 'Albatross' or the digit one? I couldn't tell from the printed list. I had to try both. Neither worked.

Next password: *Fr33ze$Fr@mes#inthe$Snow.* No luck.

Next password: *}AR{j"`L~a<ahxWX^VE8~3,~.* Ugh! Random characters. My fingers ached at the thought of typing *this* one. And it didn't work either.

I kept at it. Number forty-eight: *HorseD0gC@tIguanaGrizzly.* Obviously made up by an animal lover. Megan, perhaps? She liked animals. This one didn't work, either.

I kept at it.

Number forty-nine: *St33plechaseDolphin0nIc3.* My eyes were getting glassy as I keyed this one in and realized that I was only halfway through the list. Then, *bingo!*

With the drive unlocked, I pointed Windows Explorer to it and started to explore its contents. It was immediately obvious that this was no blank laptop waiting to be set up. I thought the best next step would be to determine if the disk were from a CIS laptop and, if so, who it belonged to. It certainly *looked* like a CIS laptop, which I quickly confirmed by checking the contents of the public desktop. The icon files in the desktop directory matched perfectly with those that CIS planted on every laptop screen.

Next, whose laptop was it? In the *users* directory, I found a subfolder with a name that corresponded to a CIS login account, the letter 'U' followed by a six-digit employee ID. I didn't have those memorized, of course, but a quick lookup on my own company laptop provided the answer: Henry Ames.

Ames! What the hell did *he* have to do with this? It did seem as if he'd been lurking around my office a lot lately. I thought he was there to BS with Rob but maybe he had another motive. And what was it about this damned disk? I resolved to find out, which meant painstakingly going through each directory on the disk and inspecting its contents. I settled in for the long haul.

For the next few hours, I pawed through file after file after file. Program files, configuration files, spreadsheets, memos, a PowerPoint presentation or two, nothing seemed out of the ordinary and certainly nothing worth murdering someone over.

I needed a break. I snapped the leash on Champ's collar and took him outside. He was improving quickly, the shaved patch on his withers where the vet stitched him was clean and healing nicely and his tail was a gentle pendulum, swinging in a large arc from side to side. I was glad to see him healing so rapidly. We took a long, slow walk in the brisk early evening air before winding up back at the condo.

Reluctantly, I tackled the disk again.

Another hour, then two, then three. This was duller even that investigating backup failures. I began to despair of finding anything that would shed any light on this whole mess, but I realized I was only halfway through the top level of the directory tree. There were many, many more folders and files to examine. I started in on the next one.

Two more hours and I couldn't take any more. I was cross-eyed and mentally exhausted. There was no way I could finish tonight so I bagged it and took a hot shower. Normally, I prefer to shower in the morning. Not tonight. The hot water worked wonders on the tension that had been building in my neck and shoulders. I toweled off and went to bed, falling asleep almost instantly.

The disk beckoned when I woke up Monday morning. I had no enthusiasm for the task, but I'd taken another personal day to continue my attack on the disk drive. I procrastinated a bit by taking Champ out. I was happy to see the dog more than ever acting like his old self.

The disk was still there when we got back.

It took real effort to sit down at the computer and resume my search. Fortified by a bagel and a can of Diet Coke, I picked up where I had left off the night before. One hour, two hours, three hours. I began to wonder if there was a better way to approach the search. Since I couldn't think of any, I continued with my mind-numbing slog.

Sometime after noon and many cans of Diet Coke later, I finally hit pay dirt when I looked in a folder named *TZXX*. Its many subfolders contained JPEG and MP4 files— pictures and videos—so I changed Explorer's display from details to thumbnails. The thumbnails appeared to show a lot of skin, so I assumed the folder was full of porn. I'm no prude and some porn wouldn't bother me, but it *was* a little dicey for a guy in InfoSec to have this kind of stuff on his company laptop. I wasn't going to raise any alarms until I confirmed my suspicions, though.

I opened one of the picture files to see if what I suspected was true, that it really was porn. The naked female in the picture looked very, very young. It was evident that she was underage and not just a flat-chested adult. Reluctantly, I looked at the next picture, then the next. They were pictures of the same girl in different poses. I tried a different folder. The girl in these pictures, also naked, was even younger than the first. She looked like she was elementary school age. Samples of JPEG files from other directories proved to be more of the same.

I shuddered and closed the picture viewer. This wasn't just porn; it was *kiddie porn!* Now things started to come into focus. Henry Ames might be worried about losing his job, but he would be much more worried about a felony conviction as a sexual offender and serving substantial prison time. Somehow, Megan got hold of his laptop and he had killed her to get it back and keep her quiet. If I had to guess, I'd say that after he killed her, he saw *her* laptop and thought it was his, the one he'd come to retrieve, and took it from her apartment. Only later did he discover that he'd swiped the wrong laptop, and that's when he took a pot shot at me. I couldn't prove any of this, but it sounded logical.

I shuddered again.

I probably should have avoided the videos and later wished I had. On the other hand, I wanted my investigation to be complete. The first one wasn't too horrible. It was simply a naked girl, underage, of course, striking different poses and gyrating for the camera. The second, one, though, was much worse. It featured a boy and a girl, both naked and both underage, apparently about to engage in some sort of sex act. I quickly hit the 'Stop' button before it got to that part. The next one was truly sickening, so much so that after I stopped it, I went to the bathroom and vomited.

I spent a long time washing my face in the sink. Then I came back, shut down the computer, and, for good measure, disconnected the disk drive. My investigation was over. I was not going to look at any more of this shit. I didn't bother buttoning up the computer case or putting it back on the floor.

Although Tosca never explicitly gave me his number, it was in my call history from the several times he had called me. I found it and punched redial.

"Joe Tosca." I was almost surprised to be reminded that he had a first name.

"Detective Tosca, this is Greg West. I have some information about that disk drive."

I explained about my search and what I had found. Simply talking about it was difficult and even Tosca seemed shaken.

"You say this punk works at your company?"

"Yes, I'm sorry to say he does. In Information Security of all places."

"You think he's distributing the stuff or just collecting it?"

"Honestly, detective, I have no idea. That's more a question for you than for me, I'd guess."

"Sure. I thought you might have an idea." I'd never heard Tosca so polite and, well, normal sounding.

"No, I don't. I'm glad to have some answers, but I wish I'd never found that shit."

"Can't blame you. Buddy of mine works vice. You should hear *his* stories."

"I think I'd rather not, detective. Certainly not tonight."

"I understand." I could hardly believe it, but I noticed a tone of sympathy in his voice. "I have some things to do on this end. Then I need to come by and pick up that drive. It belongs to the department, you know."

Being a copy, I'd assumed the drive was a throw-away. I hadn't considered that the physical hardware might belong to the Columbus Police Department.

"I'll be home all evening, detective. Come by any time."

"I think in an hour, maybe two. See you then." He sounded downright cordial when he hung up.

I couldn't concentrate on reading, television, or any other diversion. I wanted to wash those disgusting images out of my brain. I decided to see if martinis would do the trick."

I was halfway through my second martini when I heard someone tap at the door. A look through the peephole revealed that it was Tosca. I halfway expected him to send a uniform to pick up the disk like he did for the delivery, but the detective was here himself. I opened the door and motioned him in.

"Forgive my current state, detective, but I am completely, utterly, and thoroughly disgusted with humanity."

"I did a stint in Vice myself," Tosca admitted. "Some of the things you see, you can't unsee 'em."

"No, you can't. Unfortunately. What's happening now?"

"I took a couple of prowl cars out to this punk's house. Did you know he lived in a fancy neighborhood?"

"No, I had no idea where he lived."

"Apparently," he continued, "he lived there alone. By the time we got there, he'd flown the coop." He paused, then asked, "How'd you manage to crack that disk?"

I explained about the list of back door passwords Megan had given me and told him which one would unlock the encryption.

"That's going to be crucial to building a case. Of course, this is only the beginning. We have to find proof that the pictures are his and whether he's a distributor or simply a receiver and collector."

"Doesn't make much difference to me," I grumped.

"Me either. But it *does* make a difference to what he gets charged with."

"Dollars to doughnuts," I said, "he's the guy who shot at me and shot my dog."

Tosca sat for a minute before answering, "My gut tells me you're right. If we can find the gun itself, it'll be a cinch to prove it from the shell casings. But we have to find that gun."

"What should I say at work? They'll need to know something."

"Vickers and I will take care of that. I think we'll pay a call on that bigwig Battenslag in the morning and fill him in.

We're going to have to do some poking around there anyway, just to make sure nobody else in your outfit is involved.

The thought that more coworkers might be part of this was a depressing one.

"You know, not that I want to step over your investigation, but I think this explains why Megan Simmons was killed." I managed a slight smile as I said this, given Tosca's earlier insistence that I stay out of his hair.

"I bet I'm on the same page, but let's hear it." Tosca was attentive now, all traces of the hostility he exhibited in past encounters vanished.

"I think it's like this. Megan worked in Desktop Support. Somehow, Ames's laptop ended up there for repair. Maybe it was by mistake, or maybe somebody else sent it in for him. Maybe, given the fact that the support ticket and the laptop didn't match, somebody sent it in on purpose so somebody would find the shit. I don't know, but I doubt Ames himself would have done so, knowing what was on that disk, without cleaning it off."

"Unless he wasn't the one to put the stuff there in the first place."

"That's a possibility," I admitted, "but I don't think it's likely. Call it a hunch.

"Anyway, Ames found out that his laptop was in the hands of Desktop Support and that Megan was the engineer assigned to work on it. He hunted her down and killed her. I don't know for sure if she knew what was on that laptop, but odds are she did. I think that's why she hid it in my trunk instead of leaving it in her office."

Tosca was listening intently, occasionally nodding his agreement.

"Ames went to Megan's apartment. He *had* to be the Mystery Man in the videos, although he was obviously using an elaborate disguise. He's a short little penguin and it was no mean feat to dress up like a moving mountain range.

"Another thing I can't fathom is why Megan let him in. Megan was trusting but not naïve. She would never have opened her door if he'd appeared there in that Mystery Man getup. If my reasoning is correct, she knew what was on that laptop and whose laptop it was. I'm damned if I can explain why she let him in, although obviously she did.

"Megan would have fought back, too, but there were no signs of a struggle. The only way that makes sense is that he brained her right after he got in. That knocked her out, then he finished the job while she lay there immobilized. Stripping her and posing her with her arms out and legs apart was just a ruse to make it look like a sex crime."

Tosca was still silent.

"I watched the surveillance video from the apartment building," I said, "but the only person that looked out of place was the Mystery Man. I presume that you ran down all the other people in the videos?"

Tosca's eyes narrowed. "How'd *you* get hold of that video?"

"From a guy at a TV station. Did you identify the other people?"

"Took days," he said, "but we eventually did identify everyone else in the videos. Most were residents, a couple were guests. The only one we *couldn't* identify was the guy you call the Mystery Man."

"He made sure you couldn't with that outfit he wore. I'll bet he wanted to set up a big guy, probably the ex-boyfriend, as a stalking horse. It might have worked, too, if Megan hadn't kicked Murphy out the night before, although if he'd been there, Ames might have been the one on the floor instead of Megan."

"You know, West, you might not make a bad detective. I'd say your reasoning is rather good. The Simmons girl's murder showed careful planning. We couldn't find a scintilla of physical evidence placing anyone in that apartment except the dead girl and Murphy. Murphy had lived there, so that wasn't surprising, but there was nothing, absolutely nothing remotely connected to the crime scene itself that we could connect to Murphy.

"I think you're right that Ames is the guy who took a shot at you. If so, that was a panic move. I think he thought he could control the situation by killing the Simmons girl. When he saw that wasn't going to be enough, he tried a more direct method with you. He probably thought he was better with a pistol that he was. It isn't easy to hit a target in the dark a block away. And it was probably bad luck for your dog that he got hit at all."

I looked over at Champ, snoring peacefully in the corner.

"You think there's a possibility this is a mistake, or a frame-up, or some other explanation?"

"Not a chance in the world, at least not as far as the kiddie porn is concerned. I took a search warrant with me to Ames's house. I didn't stick around for the whole search, but right away they found a stack of the shit and what looked like a miniature TV studio. Looks like he made some of the stuff himself."

My skin crawled at the thought.

"You think I'm still in danger, detective?"

"Maybe, who knows. Me, I think he's a hundred miles away from here and traveling fast, probably to some place without an extradition treaty."

I agreed that this was a likely scenario.

"Well, I'll take that disk and be going. Thank you for your help with this." He looked me in the eye and added, "I mean it."

We shook hands and he left.

I shook another martini.

CHAPTER 36

Tuesday was not a productive day at work. Not long after Vickers and Tosca emerged from Jud Battenslag's office, word spread through the office like a prairie fire. It was the topic of conversation outside every cubicle, at the vending machines, and in the cafeteria. Even Brad Carter was more interested in the discussion than in work.

"Man, I *never* guessed Hank could have been involved in anything like that," Rob said. He was behaving like a hamster on cocaine, so nervous he couldn't sit still anywhere for more than a few seconds. Maybe it was because he and Henry Ames had spent so much time together lately even though they mostly talked about video games. I guessed Ames merely used that as an excuse to keep tabs on me.

"Rob," I said, "you can't know everything about everybody. He hid behind a mask. Look at that volunteer work he did, posing as Mr. Good Guy."

Brad chimed in, "This won't do the company's reputation any good once it gets out. Our stock price will probably take a hit."

"Oh," I replied, "word will get out all right. Nothing like a salacious story to grab attention."

Brad looked glum. "True enough."

"Where do you think he went?" Dexter asked.

"Don't know, don't care, as long as it's nowhere around here," I retorted.

With productivity near zero, I left work early. Although the skies were a dull gray, the temperature had warmed up a bit and I wanted to take Champ to Goodale Park again. I decided to drive to the park instead of walk. That way, if Champ got too tired, he wouldn't have to walk all the way back home. He may have been improving, but his stamina was still questionable. I found a meter on Goodale Street, parked the Mustang, and unloaded the dog.

We took a nice, slow walk around the park, stopping to pay respects to the statue of Lincoln Goodale, the park's namesake. Champ held up well and even resumed the helicopter with his tail, though at reduced velocity. When we got to the car, I loaded him in the back seat from the passenger's side, the side closer to the park. I had just shut the door and was about to walk around to the driver's side when I felt something metallic against the back of my neck.

A menacing voice growled, "All right, Greg, come on!" It was Henry Ames's voice.

Champ set up a furious barking inside the car but, with the door shut, he was effectively imprisoned. Not concerned about the dog attacking him this time, Ames led me toward a clump of trees about a hundred yards away. Rather, he piloted me, because he stayed behind me the entire time with what I assumed was the barrel of a gun pressed into my neck.

"This way!" he said and jammed the gun harder into the base of my head. The steel of the gun barrel was cold as the grave, which is where I expected to be shortly. My brain seemed paralyzed, but I concentrated as best I could on considering my options. I realized I didn't have many. I had one hundred yards, the length of a football field, to come up with something.

Twenty yards. Even with Ames poking the gun in the back of my skull, I tried to avoid walking fast. My first option was to do what he said, in which case, he'd likely kill me. He'd already killed Megan to preserve his secret and, even though the secret was out, he acted like a man with revenge on his mind.

Forty yards. I could take off running. Our encounter in Pearl Street the other night told me that Ames wasn't a crack pistol shot and I would be a moving target. On the other hand, he was shooting from a block away during the Pearl Street attack. This time he would be firing from point-blank range. The odds of him hitting me this time were much better.

Sixty yards. What if I fought him? I'd have the advantage of surprise, but it would be a small advantage compared to the one he would have being able to shoot me, again, at point-blank range. He could easily shoot before I could even turn around enough to deliver a blow.

Eighty yards. Time was running out, fast. I wondered how it felt to die this way. Would I feel anything? Would he simply wing me and let me bleed out, slowly and painfully?

Time ran out. "All right," Ames said, "this is far enough. Gimme your car keys.!" Apparently, I didn't move fast enough. "Are you fuckin' deaf? Gimme your fuckin' car keys, *right fuckin' now!*"

Despite my vulnerable position, anger welled up inside me. The guy held all the trump cards. He was going to kill me, and he was ordering me around like a slave to boot. "Fuck you, Henry." I mouthed off. "You want 'em, come get 'em." Probably not my most brilliant move because it made Ames furious.

"You shit! *You're* the one who fucked up everything for me. Now I gotta get outta here but fast and I can't even drive my own fuckin' car 'cause every prowl car in this state is looking for it."

I heard him chamber a round. I didn't *think* you felt anything when you had your head blown off, but I wasn't sure and unconsciously braced myself. A second later, there was a deafening roar. I didn't feel anything. I was still standing. I could still see and hear. Was this what it was like to be dead? Or had he simply fired a warning shot?

There was a second gunshot followed closely by a third. They were close by and made my ears ring. I turned around to see Henry Ames lying on the ground writhing and screaming in pain. He bled from a wound in his right leg but more seriously, blood flowed copiously from two holes in his abdomen. He'd dropped the gun and pressed both hands against his gut. He didn't look like much of a threat lying there, but I decided not to take any chances. I walked toward him and kicked the gun out of his reach.

I looked up and saw short, stocky man holding a large semi-automatic handgun. He sat down on the ground and gently pitched the gun out of reach.

"Call 9-1-1," was all he said.

CHAPTER 37

As I placed the call to 9-1-1, I realized it was my third such call within a month. There was nothing else to do but wait for the police to arrive. I didn't know if I should search this man, take his gun, or what. I decided that if he had wanted to kill me, he had had more than ample opportunity already and left the gun where he'd tossed it. Ames's screams of pain had become low moans and he looked like he had lost consciousness.

It felt like hours before the police showed up, but it was only minutes before one squad car, then another, and then a third skidded to the stop near my parked Mustang. The sirens cut off as the cars stopped, but their light bars still flashed brightly in the growing darkness, bathing the scene in a mixture of blue and red light that gave everything a purplish cast.

The officers immediately began to secure and process the scene. I secured permission from one of them to go release Champ. He calmed down when he saw I was okay. More police had arrived, and I took Champ back to where a knot of them had gathered. I heard one uniform tell another that an ambulance was on the way, to which the second officer opined that Ames needed a meat wagon instead of an ambulance. Glancing at the now-still figure lying on the ground, I suspected the second cop was right.

The next few minutes were a blur of activity. Cops were stringing up crime scene tape. Other cops were scouring the park for witnesses. Police radios gargled in the distance. An ambulance arrived and loaded a now motionless Henry Ames before racing off toward Grant Hospital, with lights flashing and siren screaming. I took advantage of this breather to text Jenna a very brief outline of what had happened and assured her I was unhurt. I didn't want her to panic if one of the TV stations got a "breaking news" alert on the air before I had a chance to talk to her. I also told her I would be by later.

As the adrenaline began to leave my body, I realized I was physically and mentally drained. I'd come frighteningly close to dying. The guy with the pistol had intervened, rescuing me, but Ames was either dead or badly wounded. Neither of these was a pleasant prospect. The police would eventually sort it all out. I was just waiting for the investigators, who I knew would want to talk with me, but I wished I were far away from Goodale Park.

"*You* again?" It was Tosca's voice, his tough-cop act failing to mask what I sensed was genuine concern.

"Yes, detective, I'm afraid it *is* me again," I responded wearily.

Vickers was with him and I briefly explained what had happened. Vickers stayed with me while Tosca went to interview the man who shot Ames. He was still sitting quietly in the same spot he'd sat in after tossing away the gun.

"Joe told me about the disk drive," she said flatly.

"I can't think of an experience I've had in my life so far that was worse than seeing that filth," I responded. "It left me numb—and sick."

"Was that the guy the ambulance carted off?"

"Yes, it was. I thought he'd blown town. I think Detective Tosca though so, too. I didn't expect him to sneak up on me like that."

"He dropped off the radar," she said, "and we all believed he'd fled, probably somewhere that didn't have an extradition treaty with us. We had his house staked out and he never showed up there. He had almost eighteen hours before you found the dead girl. If he was going to bug out, I don't know why he didn't use that time to do it."

"He didn't," I replied, "because after killing Megan, he thought he was out of the woods. Then he discovered that he'd taken the wrong laptop and that *his* laptop with the kiddie porn on it was still floating around."

"I guess that makes sense," Vickers said.

"Think he'll make it?" I asked.

"I don't know. I didn't see him. Officer Strozic thinks the guy was dead when they loaded him into the ambulance, and Strozic has enough experience that I'd trust his instincts."

"Might be for the best, all things considered," I mused.

"Maybe."

Tosca came back and joined us. "Another sick part of this whole story that was already sick enough to begin with. That guy over there, he's just some poor schmo. Says he knew this Ames punk was producing kiddie porn because Ames had used the guy's daughter in some of it. She was thirteen. Ames told her he was going to get her a modeling contract. When she found out what was going on, it was too late. She couldn't get away. Afterward, she killed herself; got hold of some pills and put herself to sleep, permanently."

I wanted to vomit again but somehow managed to keep my stomach in check.

"Says he's been following the guy," Tosca continued, "looking for an opportunity. He didn't figure the courts would do enough to Ames, so he decided to act on his own. Said he hadn't picked the park, that he was just following the guy. When he saw Ames was about to off you, he decided to step in."

"That's pitiful beyond words," I said. "It makes me want to both cry *and* puke. Think there's any truth in it?"

"Can't say for sure, but when you've interviewed as many people as Sharona and I have, you get to have a pretty good idea of who's telling you the truth and who's trying to pump sunshine up your skirt. We'll interview him formally downtown, but I think his story's on the up-and-up."

"May I go, detectives? I'm drained, I need to take my dog home, and I *really* need to see my girlfriend so that she knows I'm okay."

"I don't see any reason for you to stick around here," Vickers said. She looked at Tosca and he nodded agreement. "Go on home. If we need you for anything, we'll call you."

"Thanks," was all I could muster the energy to say.

I led Champ back to the car and, once again, loaded him into the back seat. This time, I carefully looked over my shoulder before closing the passenger door. There was nobody there. In no time, I was in the driver's seat and the Mustang was speeding the short distance home.

CHAPTER 38

Jenna was waiting for me when Champ and I walked in. She and I had exchanged keys, so I was not surprised to see here waiting in my living room. She jumped out of her chair when I opened the door and, by the time Champ and I were inside, she had run over and thrown her arms around me in a huge bear hug. I felt moisture on my neck that I realized was from tears.

"God, I was so *scared!* When you texted me, I imagined all *sorts* of things happening to you. I was afraid I was going to lose you!" When she looked up at me, it was obvious she'd been crying.

"Jenna," I said, "I hope this is the end of it. I'm not planning to go anywhere, not for a while at any rate. I'm sorry I caused you so much worry." She buried her face in my shoulder and sobbed gently. I lifted her chin and lightly kissed her. "Jenna, it's going to be all right, I know it."

I told her what happened in the park, sparing her none of the details. She visibly shuddered when I described the gun barrel to the back of my head. Tears flowed again when I told her about the man who shot Ames and the heartbreaking story of his abused daughter. I held her tight and let her cry herself out.

"I can't even imagine how people can be that awful," she said. She looked up at me with red-rimmed eyes. "I mean, that man's daughter, she was just a *child!* And now a life is wasted because she was scared and made a panicked decision she couldn't undo."

"To tell the truth, when Tosca told me that story, I had to work really hard not to throw up. It *is* sickening. And what's even worse is that I worked with the guy for years and never suspected. Too bad these guys don't have a sign on their forehead that says, 'child molester.'"

"We have people come into the hospital that look perfectly normal but later you find out that they've been involved in some really weird shit. More so when I worked critical care than the cardiac unit, though. Point is the old cliché about not judging a book by its cover is really true."

"I just hope this is the end," I said, meaning every word. "I suppose Tosca and Vickers will want to follow up with me, but I'm thinking—hoping—this is the last we see of this whole sordid business. Megan deserves to rest in peace."

"Yes, she does," Jenna replied simply. "And you—we— need some peace, too."

Jenna slept at my place that night. Several times during the night I felt her reach over and lightly touch me, as if to reassure herself that I was still there. I guess the last few weeks had been as traumatic for her as for me.

Despite the day's ordeal, I slept well that night, just knowing that Jenna was here with me gave me a relaxing inner peace.

CHAPTER 39

Jenna and I both took Wednesday off. I was starting to get concerned that I'd burned though my PTO, but Brad told me not to worry about it. Jenna had a sizable PTO balance, so we'd planned a lazy day together. Other than doing our laundry together, we did little else. I had just poured two glasses of a very robust Cabernet when my phone rang. It was Tosca. This time, though, my gut didn't clinch.

"Good afternoon, Detective." I tried my best to make my voice genuinely friendly.

"Good afternoon yourself, West." All traces of the detective's earlier hostility had vanished. "I was wondering if you'd mind if I came by this afternoon. I have a few things to wrap up before I can close this case."

"Not at all. I assumed you'd want to have a follow-up interview. I'm glad it's not at Headquarters, though."

"Naw, we don't need to go formal, but I did want to drop by if that's okay."

"By all means. I plan to be here all afternoon doing nothing but enjoying a fine red wine."

Tosca suppressed a chuckle as he answered, "You're one of a few stops I have to make, but I'll be there before dark. Bye." He hung up.

"Jenna," I said, "Detective Tosca is going to grace us with his presence this afternoon."

"Do you want me to go?"

"Most assuredly not."

She seemed pleased. "Good. I've wanted to meet this guy."

Thinking about how my relationship with the detective had morphed over the last few days, I said, "He's the kind of guy that tries to protect himself with a very hard crust on the outside, but inside, he's a decent person. And I agree with Ty Jackson, the TV cameraman. I've come to think he's a rather good detective."

Jenna smiled. "Sounds like a *very* interesting guy. That's why I want to meet him in person and see what *my* intuition tells me."

We folded laundry between sips of wine. We had put the last of the clean clothes away, mine in my closet and drawers, Jenna's in baskets to take to her place, when we heard a knock at the door. A look though the peephole confirmed it was Tosca.

"Detective, don't you ever take a day off?" I asked, only partly humorously.

"Rarely," he shot back.

"Jenna, I'd like you to meet Detective Joe Tosca, of the Columbus Police Department. Detective Tosca, this is my friend—my girlfriend—Jenna Stone."

The two shook hands and swiftly appraised each other. "Nice to meet you, Miss Stone."

"Likewise, Detective."

"Unless you're on duty," I said, "would you care to join us in a glass of wine."

"Normally, I'm a beer guy, but today wine sounds fine. And no, I'm not on duty. This is my last stop."

I produced another glass, poured, and offered it to the detective. He raised and said, "To you two lovebirds." Out of the corner of my eye, I thought I saw Jenna blush slightly.

"Thank you. I guess this case helped bring us together." I pulled Jenna to my side and gave her a little squeeze.

"If you're up for it," Tosca said, "I can give you a rundown on what we've managed to dig up."

"Yes, I think I'd be interested in hearing that," I said. Jenna nodded.

"The guy in the park with the gun, his story checked out," Tosca began. "His name is Shawn Nettles. He and his wife divorced several years ago. She had drug problems, bad problems, and he ended up with sole custody of his daughter, Laura. Nobody knows where the mother is or if she's even still alive. We don't really see the need to spend manpower trying to trace her.

"Anyway, Nettles said the daughter was really pretty. He showed us some pictures and I'd have to agree. She was thirteen but looked older. Nettles says she'd always dreamed of being a model and that's how this punk Ames snared her. He promised to hook her up with a modeling agency but said he'd need some sample photos first. The photo shoot was to take place at his house. She objected when she found out he meant *nude* photos, but by then she was trapped in the place and had no way to get out and get home.

"Ames managed to get her undressed, then he sprang another shocker: she was going to have to have sex while he filmed her. Ames had to drug her to make that happen. Then he sent her home in a cab that *she* had to pay for. She was ashamed of what she'd done and embarrassed that he'd duped her. Hard to imagine how tough that would be for a kid who was barely a teenager to handle.

"Nettles was at work when the daughter came home. He doesn't know where she got the sleeping pills, says he never kept stuff like that around the house because of what happened with his wife. By the time he got home, the daughter was dead. She left a note that spilled the whole story, almost. Her note told *what* happened but not *who* or *where*. It wasn't my case, but I talked to the detective whose case it was. He tried, really tried, to find something to link a suspect to the girl but he came up empty. This is the kind of case that really gets you in the gut, so I know he did the absolute best he could.

"Nettles said he was cleaning out some of his daughter's old stuff and ran across her diary. The entry for the day she died simply said, "Henry Ames, 1:30. Once he had a name and looked up where he lived, it rang a bell with something he read in the suicide note. He figured that Ames was the guy and started stalking him."

"He didn't contact the police?"

"No. By that time, he'd convinced himself that nothing the law did would be enough for Mr. Henry Ames. He followed him, and he had a gun, but I don't think he really had a solid plan to kill him. You know how rattlesnakes are supposed to be able to mesmerize a rabbit? I think Ames had that same effect on Nettles. He probably had plenty of chances to shoot the guy and passed on 'em. But he was confused. Then when he saw Ames about to shoot *you*, he decided to intervene. He aimed his first shot low, but when Ames pointed his gun at *him*, he went for the body mass. I guess Nettles is a decent pistol shot."

"Don't take this the wrong way, detective," I replied, "but the conversations we've been having lately make me physically sick." That was no lie. My stomach was churning.

"No offense taken. This is some really sick stuff. I couldn't handle a steady diet of it. That's why I transferred from Vice to Homicide.

"What's going to happen to Nettles?" I asked.

"The D.A. will have to charge him with something. Regardless of the provocation, you can't have guys running around using a pistol to get private justice. Under the circumstances, though, it probably won't be first degree. He *did* prevent Ames from killing you, after all."

"Has he got a lawyer?"

"Yeah, guy named Behan. He's got an office down in the Brewery District. Nettles told us everything, though, even after he retained counsel. Behan tried to get him to shut up, but he wouldn't. He wanted to get the story out. Based on circumstances, the lawyer might have a shot at diminished capacity or something."

"Detective Tosca, I wouldn't be sitting here right now if Shawn Nettles hadn't shot Ames. I am going to see that lawyer and offer to do anything, absolutely *anything* I can to help Nettles now." Jenna silently nodded her agreement.

"I understand. I don't blame you, and I have no objections." Tosca grinned. This was probably the first time he had anything approaching a smile on his face in years.

"Some other things you might want to know. We were all over Ames' house like white on rice and we found a couple of things. He had three sets of stilts, which could explain how he was able to look so tall on the surveillance video, and a fat suit, which could explain the bulk. We also found a cowboy hat that looked a lot like the one in the video, although the images aren't quite good enough to make a positive match. It may or may not have been *the* hat; it didn't have any blood on it. Anyway, to me, one cowboy hat looks like another. We didn't find the coat, though.

"When we pulled his credit card accounts, we found that he'd rented a car in Fort Mitchell, Kentucky. That's just across the river from Cincinnati in case you didn't know."

"I do know," I replied.

"We also found a surveillance video from a building a couple of doors down from the apartment building. It shows a guy who *looked* like Ames getting into a car that *looked* like the one he rented. The video was too grainy to be sure about Ames and it didn't show the car's license plate clearly enough to positively identify it. The guy in the video was carrying a big bundle that he put in the trunk. We got the Fort Mitchell cops to impound the car the rental company said he rented, so we may eventually get some evidence."

"How did he get out of Megan's building without being seen on the video?"

"No way to tell for sure," the detective said. "Fire escape, maybe, or maybe over the roof.

"Oh, and the gun he had at the park? It was the gun that fired those shots on Pearl Street, so you were right about that."

"But no proof he killed Megan?" I inquired.

"Not yet. But I'm betting we'll find something in that rental car."

"I sure hope so. I'm sure he's the killer, but I'd feel better with some concrete proof."

"You and me both," Tosca agreed.

One thing still nagged me. "How did Ames get into Megan's apartment? It sure *looks* like she let him in, and she didn't put up a fight."

Tosca paused for a minute, then said, "Unless we can dig up a witness that saw something, we're stuck with speculation. Vickers and I canvassed that building thoroughly and came up dry, so I don't expect any new witnesses to show up. Maybe he talked his way in with a yarn about explaining how he was innocent. Maybe she left the door open long enough for him to sneak in. It's even possible he got hold of a key somehow and surprised her. I just don't know for sure."

Finishing his wine, the detective stood up, held out his hand, and we shook. Then he shook hands with Jenna.

"Nice to meet you, Miss Stone," he said to Jenna. To me, "Take care of yourself, West. You seem to have a knack for getting into trouble."

"Detective Tosca, I hope to stay as far away from trouble as the moon is from the sun." I meant that quite literally. I'd had enough danger and excitement for several lifetimes.

"So long, West, and you, too, Miss Stone," he said, as he left the condo and quietly closed the door behind him.

"I think you've pegged Mr. Detective Tosca pretty accurately," Jenna said. "I'll bet anything that hard shell he showed you hides a sensitive man inside. Nurses have a way of seeing things in people that others don't."

About an hour before sunset, it began to snow outside. We turned out the lights and cuddled under a blanket on the sofa as we watched big flakes cover the rooftops with fluffy white. As it got dark, we started making out. Before long, we were in bed making love.

CHAPTER 40

There was one more thing I felt I had to do. I had to see Liam Murphy again and tell him how things had played out. He had been close to Megan, and a suspect to boot, so I thought knowing the whole story might give him some closure.

I reached Manny's just before 6:00 and, sure enough, there was the redheaded giant holding down a stool at the center of the bar. The place looked almost as it had on my previous visits, except that Ms. Nondescript was nowhere in sight. Today there was a kid behind the bar with huge gauges in both ears and tattoos peeking out from under his shirt sleeves. He must have been over 21 to be behind the bar but he didn't look it.

I sat down beside Murphy and ordered a draft Budweiser. Seeing that his can was empty, I ordered him another PBR as well. "Good evening, Liam," I said as a conversational opening.

He looked over at me. "Hiya, Mr. West." At least he remembered my name this time. His green eyes weren't hostile today, though. Instead, they looked sad and full of regret. Undoubtedly still thinking about Megan, I supposed.

"Have you heard the news?"

"What news?" he asked.

"We found Megan's killer."

Murphy's eyes widened, so I quickly added, "He's dead."

"Yeah?"

"Yes, I thought you'd like to hear about it, you having been close to Megan and all, not to mention being arrested as a suspect twice."

"So who was it that done it?"

"His name," I said, "was Henry Ames. He worked at the same company as Megan and me."

"Why?"

It was a simple question. The answer was simple, too, but it wouldn't be anything but painful.

I said, "He was into some bad stuff. Child pornography. He collected it. He sold it. He even *made* it. Megan found out. He had some on a laptop that somebody sent to her for repair. He killed her to keep her quiet."

Murphy's face showed his disgust and he said, "That's a helluva note!"

"Yes, it is. And he almost killed me, too."

I told him about Shawn Nettles and my narrow escape.

"Damn! Was this guy some kinda badass?"

"Not really. He was just a dumpy, nerdy-looking guy. I worked with him—not closely, you understand—for years and never suspected he was involved in kiddie porn."

"Guess he kinda got what was comin' to him. But it still don't bring Megan back."

"No, it doesn't."

"Ya know, my brother Sean always tole me I didn't deserve Megan, that she was too good for me. Maybe he was right." He turned his head away quickly and started examining his beer can intently. "I guess she and me weren't meant to be together."

"I'm sorry, Liam."

"Thanks for tellin' me about this."

"I thought you should know. Maybe it'll help you deal with it some."

He turned back toward me and I saw his eyes were moist.

"I miss her. Wish I'd been there when this creep showed up. Can't do nothin' 'bout it now, though."

He threw back his head and drained the last of his can of Pabst. I finished my beer, laid a twenty on the bar, and got up to leave.

"It's never easy losing somebody you care about," I said, thinking about Lisa. But life doesn't stop, and we have to keep plugging away. You'll do fine, Liam—eventually. So long."

"Bye, Mr. West."

I left him there, a redheaded giant alone with his thoughts.

CHAPTER 41

I was walking along a deserted white sand beach holding hands with Lisa. She was the pretty 22-year-old graduate student I married thirty-odd years ago. We often vacationed at the seashore because Lisa adored beaches. She found peace and relaxation in the vast stretches of sand and water, which is ironic considering the immense energy boiling up from the oceans. I never was much of a beach person myself, but I saw how much Lisa enjoyed beaches and drew strength from them, so I went along. Now, as the two of us walked along the wet sand leaving bare footprints behind us, I listened to the quiet roar of the surf and felt a tranquility that I'd never got from a beach before. Lisa laughed as the saltwater lapped gently around her feet.

We walked quietly for a time, she relishing the water and I lost in thought. Finally, I got the courage to speak. "Lisa," I began, "I want to tell you something. I've—"

She put her hand to my lips and said, "Shh! I know what you're going to say. It's okay." Her voice was quiet and low. I strained to hear her words above the sound of the surf as she continued. "I loved you, Greg. We had a wonderful life and I loved you as much as a woman can. But I can't be with you anymore. I can't love you *now*."

"But—"

She silenced me again. "I said it's okay. You were terribly, terribly lonely after I left. I *know* how lonely you were. Since we can't be together, I sent Jenna to you. Be as good to her as you were to me."

Then she was gone, and I was alone on an empty beach.

My eyes opened and I realized it had been a dream. Beside me, Jenna slept quietly, her soft, regular breathing barely audible.

Now, I finally and fully understood. Lisa's love for me and mine for her had been generous and unselfish. Both of us wanted the best for the other no matter what. Lisa had been taken from me and I sorely missed her, but she wanted me to be happy. Lisa wanted me to have a life with Jenna.

I turned over and, careful not to wake her, gently slid my arm around Jenna's waist.

George Pallas Author Bio

George Pallas was born in Chattanooga, Tennessee and grew up in the Nashville area. He moved to Ohio after graduating from Vanderbilt University and began a career in information technology. After retiring from the IT industry, he turned to writing.

As a writer, George has two short stories to his credit *Stalking Horse* is his first book. George also writes about historical true crime in his blog, *Old Crime is New Again* at https://georgepallas.com/.

George lives in downtown Columbus, Ohio with his wife, Sharon, and his dog, Sheldon Cooper.